Animal Ghost Stories

Animal Ghost Stories

Collected and Retold by
Nancy Roberts

Published 1995 by August House, Inc.,
P.O. Box 3223, Little Rock, Arkansas, 72203,
501-372-5450.

Printed in the United States of America

10 9 8 7 6 5 4 3 2 1   PB

LIBRARY OF CONGRESS CATALOGING-IN-PUBLICATION DATA
Roberts, Nancy, 1924-
Animal ghosts / collected and retold by Nancy Roberts.
p.   cm.
Includes bibliographical references.
ISBN 0-87483-401-5 (alk. paper)
1. Animal ghosts.
I. Title.
BF1484.R63   1995
133.1'4--dc20   95-13039

Executive editor: Liz Parkhurst
Project editor: Rufus Griscom
Design director: Ted Parkhurst
Cover art and illustrations: David Boston
Cover design: Harvill Ross Studios, Ltd.

The paper used in this publication meets the minimum requirements of
the American National Standard for Information Sciences—
Permanence of Paper for Printed Library Materials, ANSI Z39.48-1984.

AUGUST HOUSE, INC.   PUBLISHERS   LITTLE ROCK

Contents

Introduction

PEOPLE OFTEN ASK ME why I write ghost stories. Freelancing for *The Charlotte Observer*, I wrote the story of the ghost of a young woman in a black lace dress who appeared on the stairs in a pre-Civil War home in Fayetteville, North Carolina. Later, the features editor asked me to write similar ghost stories from all over the state. I found them fascinating.

While this series was running in the paper, a reporter went up to Flat Rock, North Carolina, to do a story on Carl Sandburg.

In the course of the interview, Mr. Sandburg was kind enough to mention that he liked the ghost story series. He sent me this message:

"Tell the lady who writes the ghost stories for the paper that they should be published in a book."

Hearing from Mr. Sandburg was the next thing to receiving a message from God. I found a publisher and a book was born—the first of twenty-four. Ten were collections of ghost stories, all of which are still in print, and the remaining fourteen were on other subjects. Though all of latter are now out of print, three of them received good reviews in the *New York Times*. None of the ghost story collections has ever received such a distinction, but I'm comforted that they are still in print.

Prior to this book, I had written only two stories about animals: the "Hound of Goshen" from *Ghosts of the Carolinas* and "Specter of the Sorrel Stallion" from *Southern Ghosts*. I have always loved animals and I don't know why I didn't write more about them sooner.

I can recall longing for a pet goat as a child and finally phoning a local farmer to ask him to "please deliver one with a beard." Unfortunately my parents overheard the call and cancelled the order, but our home was never without dogs and cats. Our blue Persian, Dawn, a gift to mother from dad, emerged from his crate angry and bedraggled after a harrowing trip from Texas to Wisconsin. Later Dawn reluctantly shared his domain with a chow puppy named I Ching.

I Ching and I frolicked noisily through the house in games of hide-

and-seek, and miraculously he was able to find me even when I had hidden in a built-in cupboard four feet off the floor. I believe that I had a unique, wordless communication with this warm, affectionate, playful animal. Some reader may say, "Yes, the olfactory language," but it was more than that. Unfortunately, I Ching died of distemper before the vaccine was discovered. I can still remember the sadness of our family the first night after his death. No one could talk. Supper went largely uneaten.

When people have asked me what I have been working on recently, I have replied, "A book about animal ghost stories." It has been surprising how often someone has then said, "I know one." Usually such stories are about the ghosts of animals that a family member has seen.

Why did I include the stories about strange creatures? In what other company but ghosts would the story of the famous "Jersey Devil," the plat-eye of the southeastern coast, the South Carolina "Lizard Man," or the "Ogopogo" of British Columbia be at home? Like ghosts, they too are mysterious and appear only at their own inclination. It is up to the reader to judge credibility.

But let's return to the familiar animals. I recall talking with a retired minister about the death of his favorite dog, and I asked him, "Do you think we will see our pets in the next world?"

His reply was, "Nancy, if their presence in heaven will make you happy, I think they will be there."

May these stories have a special meaning for animal lovers everywhere.

PET GHOSTS

Angie's Dog Always

THE MOUNTAIN FOLK didn't know what to make of Dr. Gaine Cannon at first. All they had heard was that the stranger had left a good practice in another state because he wanted to come up to an isolated community here in the North Carolina mountains and build a hospital. It didn't seem to make sense. He was probably nothing but a dreamer.

They were used to traveling twenty-five miles over precipitous, winding, one-lane dirt roads to the nearest medical facility at Brevard. Of course, it was too far for those who lived in the more remote reaches of the mountains who couldn't always get to it in time, even if they had a car or a phone to call an ambulance. They just died if the heart attack was too bad or if the appendix ruptured. Even if they could get there in time the cost of a hospital was out of the question for families living on three or four thousand dollars a year like most folks did way back in the coves and hollows.

Dr. Gaine Cannon knew all that when he moved up to Balsam Grove near Rosman, but he was of mountain stock himself, and he cared about these people. He would have been the last one to think of himself as some kind of maverick, yet in some ways, that's what he was.

Today, bouncing along in his black Jeep over the gravel road to his clinic, Dr. Cannon noticed the darkening sky over the purple ridges. A warning flutter of snowflakes melted upon his windshield. He was glad he had no calls to make that day. While the hospital was taking shape here in this sheltered valley, Doc Cannon was living in a combination home-clinic. The problem of what material to use for the hospital exterior walls had been easy to solve. Seeing the soft browns and ochers of the smooth stones in the mountain stream near his clinic, he knew they were what he wanted to use. Patients were asked to bring a load of rocks from a streambed near them when they could not pay his fee, and wagonloads of rocks had arrived.

11

The snow was falling faster, and Cannon started his windshield wiper.

Walls were already raised for the Albert Schweitzer Memorial Hospital. A pretentious name? Not necessarily, for he and Dr. Schweitzer had become fast friends during the summer Doc Cannon spent working with him at his hospital in Africa. The inspiration of Dr. Schweitzer kindled Cannon's desire for a similar ministry to the people of Appalachia. He had a pretty good idea what his income would be even before he brought his dream to Balsam Grove, but he didn't seem to worry about his patients not having money to pay. If it was not river stones, they paid him in whatever coin they could—a home-cured ham from their smokehouse, fresh vegetables or occasionally a jug of "mountain dew."

An old man walking beside the road raised one gnarled, arthritic hand to hail him, and Cannon slowed the Jeep.

"They's two people gone up to your clinic, Doc. One looked like he was 'bout to die. Said he got hold of some bad corn liquor. T'other man didn't say if anything was ailin' him."

"I'm on my way home now, Rufus. I'll see to 'em. How's that high blood of yours." Behind his thick spectacles, Doc's round, bright eyes stared at the other man with concern. "Want me to check it for you?"

"Naw. It's not botherin' me. 'Course I can't stay away from some country ham now and agin," he admitted with a shamefaced grin.

"I've got that problem, too, Rufus."

"Looks like we're going to get a heavy snow," said Rufus McCall motioning toward dark gray clouds to the west. It was coming down harder now.

"Want me to run you home?"

"Nope. The house ain't that fur."

Doc Cannon nodded and went on. Hanging a right turn, he took the narrow dirt road to his clinic. An old Chevy was drawn up near the front porch and inside it sat the Tollivers. Or rather Tom sat, and Ben slumped over against the passenger side door. It was pretty much like Rufus had said.

He did what he could for the sick man.

"You got hold of some bad corn, Tom. Could have killed you this time," said Doc. "Who made it?"

There was no answer.

"You drink any of it, Ben?"

"Nope. Ain't nothin' wrong with me, Doc."

"All right."

"Did you know Annie Neal's little Angie is bad sick?"

"No, I didn't. They are over in Jackson County. Been there many a time."

"Yep. I heard it from Annie's husband, Luther, at the store this morning."

"Well, why in tarnation didn't Luther come for me, then?"

"Cause he ain't much account. You know that, Doc."

Doc Cannon shook his head in frustration, his lips compressed.

"Think you could get over there, Doc?"

"Ben, it's going to snow and maybe keep on all night. You know what that road's like up to the Hughes place. I might just slide right off the side of the mountain!"

"Mmmn," sighed Ben. "Reckon you're right. But that Angie's shore a sweet li'l old thing."

This was unreasonable when Luther Hughes hadn't even bothered to come or send for him, thought Cannon, but he found himself responding to the indictment in Ben's voice.

"If it begins to snow hard, Ben, I can't promise I'll even see the turnoff to get up to their cabin."

The Tolliver brothers climbed into the junkyard Chevy which coughed, died, and then started uncertainly. Doc Cannon looked after them, frowning.

He heated some coffee and warmed the plate of "mountain britches" beans, ham, and cornbread his nurse, Helen, had prepared for him before she left. As he ate he debated whether he should try to go to the Hughes place. Helen had once said, "You're all the time worrying about your patients or thinking about your work. I don't wonder you haven't got any time left for a woman."

Helen must have been right. For him marriage had been like a Sunday suit he was always uncomfortable wearing or shoes he couldn't quite get broken in. The divorce had to have been his fault, he thought, sighing. He thought about work too much; and he settled back in his chair to read the Brevard paper.

He scanned the local news for about thirty minutes then glanced out the window. The snow had stopped, and he ought to be able to get up that road to the Hughes place. If they just had a phone he could call and ask them to put some kind of flag out where the road branched off to their cabin, but he would recognize it anyway. He wasn't too worried about getting stuck. The new snow tires on the Jeep should make it.

Opening the glass cupboard doors in his small office pharmacy, he selected an assortment of medications and placed them in his bag. He snapped the worn black leather case shut and sat down, jerking his boots off and tugging on a second pair of wool socks. With a heavy red and black wool blanket coat around his ample figure and an old bandanna knotted around his neck, Doc climbed into the Jeep.

A scant inch of snow coated the red clay road—nothing to worry about yet. But when he reached Jackson County it began to snow again, and it was harder to see any distance. The Jeep lurched through potholes and along deep rock-laden ruts on the dirt road. It was one lane and narrow. If he had to pass he would only be able to do so where the road widened as it branched off to some isolated cabin. Driving this road in summer, he had often looked out the window on his left and down a drop of several hundred feet. He knew that the blue abyss was right beside him now even though the curtain of falling snow blocked a view of it. Not being able to see made the drive almost easier than driving on a clear day, but he found himself leaning inward toward the mountain, hugging the side of it with his Jeep.

Out of habit he blew the horn before he inched cautiously around each looping curve, although most people would be at home by the fire today. He thought about Angie, hoped he wasn't too late and hoped he had brought everything in his bag that she might need.

The Jeep gave a wrenching jolt, pitched down six or eight inches, bounced up again, and continued up the incline. That would be one of the creek beds—no bridges on this road. Then, five minutes later, he felt the front wheels dropping again. He was crossing a second creek. How did the school bus ever get up here in weather like this? He knew the answer to that one: it didn't. He opened the driver's side window and occasionally leaned his head out to see. Snowflakes began to freeze on his lashes, and his face felt stiff and numb. He began searching for the turnoff to the Hughes place. It must have started snowing much earlier up here for the dark limbs of the firs were heavy with their white burdens, and drifts curved up like cresting waves on the side of the road toward the mountain.

It was only midafternoon but from the light it could have been dusk. He began to feel his isolation in this white world of snowy, swirling flakes as he realized that he could easily pass the road—actually no more than a logging trail—leading to the house. Now he could see only a few feet beyond the length of the Jeep. Where was the grove of eerie, wind-twisted trees on the left just before the Hughes turnoff? Had he missed it? Would he get there tonight to treat Angie or would he freeze to death?

Now, seldom given to attending services in any of the small, white frame churches nearby, he found himself saying, "Jesus, Jesus, Jesus!" under his breath in a kind of prayer—more for Angie than himself. He had been present at the little church near the clinic each Sunday morning until the minister had thrown him out for admitting his doubts about the literal meaning of the story of Jonah and the whale.

A faint sound came from behind the Jeep. He heard it again, and backed up a little, very cautiously. Through his open window, along with snow, came the barking of a dog, sharp, insistent. Then he saw him. He would have known that dog anywhere. A dog that looked like a cross between a golden retriever and a large coon dog stood beside the road, a long reddish fringe of fur hanging from the underside of his snowy tail. It was Angie's dog. He backed up a little more. The animal kept barking, coming toward him a few paces, then striking out on a trail among the trees. Gaine cut the wheel recklessly toward the slope of the mountain and followed. He hoped to God this was the road.

Gratefully he felt the tires of the Jeep settle into shallow ruts, the dog always keeping about twenty feet ahead. Then, in a clearing, he saw the dark shape of the little house. What luck! The dog had led him right to it.

A deep, fluffy blanket of snow lay on the slab steps up to the front door, and there was no sign of footprints. He knocked but did not receive an answer. With a sick child someone ought to be at home, he thought testily. He stepped back and looked up. A serpent of blue smoke curled lazily upward from the stone chimney, so he put his hand on the knob. Suddenly the door was opened by Mrs. Hughes, and he almost fell into the room.

There was quick, grateful recognition in Mrs Hughes' eyes.

"Doc! I sure near didn't hear you out there. Come in."

The air in the room was close, filled with the smoky scent of the wood fire. Dr. Cannon kneeled down beside a golden-haired child who lay near it on a pallet of quilts and placed his stethoscope against her chest. Eyes bright and face flushed, her little body almost burned his hand—pneumonia. Had he reached her in time? He gave her a shot. She stirred and then was up on one elbow trying to rise.

"Did you see him, Doc?" she said excitedly.

He tried to ease her back down on the pillow. "See who, honey?"

"My Prince."

Doc Cannon glanced questioningly at her mother.

"She meant her dog, Prince. It's just the fever talking, Doc," and she clasped Angie's hand tenderly in hers. "Hush. You know you didn't really see Prince, honey. You dreamt it. Now go to sleep."

"But I did see him, Momma," Angie exclaimed. "I saw him waving his tail as he trotted along the road up to the house here, and then he came in the room and over to my bed. He licked my face. He did, Momma."

Dr. Cannon smiled. "He's a fine dog."

Her mother put a finger up to her lips and gave Dr. Cannon a look of warning that puzzled him.

"Tell me. Is she going to be all right, Doctor Cannon?"

Angie was on a pallet a few feet away and could hear her. She did not want to argue with the child whose belief in the presence of the dog seemed to be making her feel better.

"Yes, I think she's going to be OK, but you send for me, now, if she takes a turn for the worse."

At the door of the cabin, Gaine Cannon handed her a paper packet of pills for Angie.

"By the way, as far as I'm concerned, Annie Neal, that dog ought to have a medal. I had already missed the road that leads up here when I heard him barking. There he was standing at the edge of the forest, so I turned the Jeep around, and he struck off into what seemed like nowhere to me with all the snow. I couldn't be sure he wasn't hunting down a rabbit but I followed him. The dog led me all the way up to your cabin."

Annie Neal's face stared at Gaine Cannon with a mixture of amazement and discomfort.

"What's the matter? Did I say something to upset you?"

"Doc, Prince was killed by a car almost a month ago."

"Killed!"

"Yes, down on the highway. Angie's father, Luther, carved a wooden plank in the shape of a grave rock for Prince. He said it was all foolishment, but the child took on so, he went ahead and carved some words she wrote herself. Angie plumb loved that dog."

Mrs. Hughes looked out the door and up at the sky. "Snow's stopped. Maybe you'll see the marker when you go out. Prince's grave is at the edge of the woods where you turn into our place."

"It's getting on toward night, Annie Neal, but I'll see it when I come back to check on Angie."

"Doc, do you think it really could have been Prince?" asked Annie Neal quietly. "He was the only dog I ever saw all the way up here, and there's not another house for five miles."

"I don't know."

"Well, however you got here," she said, "I want to thank you, Doc." She thrust a jug of apple cider into his arms. "Take this for now and I aim to see you get some river stones for your hospital when Luther goes to Brevard."

As he drove down the mountain Gaine Cannon thought about his experiences of the past few years—balls of fire rolling down the roof of a home where a man lay dying, lights drifting eerily in and out among the headstones of a cemetery he once passed. The mystery of Prince's appearance and help in finding the Hughes' cabin would join a handful of other unexplained events during his family medical practice here in the Appalachians.

Though he was eager to get off the mountain before dark, he saw the marker and could not help braking. There the makeshift memorial to the dog stood beneath a big tree. Leaving the motor running, the doctor got out and plodded through the snow. He stopped in front of it and untied the bandanna scarf from his neck to flick the snow from the face of the board. The words he read were crudely carved:

PRINCE
Angie's dog always.

The Hounds of Merrywood

ANGUS GILLESPIE HAD AT FIRST enjoyed living in Connecticut with its beautiful, gently rolling countryside and quaint historic towns, but after ten years he and his artist wife decided that they wanted fresh vistas. Diane had vowed she would go mad if she painted one more old, typically New England barn. "But I'd still like something countrified and quiet," she said. Angus agreed.

Leafing through a magazine on rural property, Angus found himself drawn to estate advertisements from Virginia. As a literary agent he could live a reasonable distance from New York City and take a shuttle to his office three or four days a week. The winters might be milder, too. He began to read the listings.

Suddenly he saw one that intrigued him.

> Escape the urban rat race for a rural Eden. The "Merrywood," 2-story colonial country home, formal dining room, 4.5 baths, 5 bedrooms, large master bedroom, modern kitchen. Pool, tennis court. Your family deserves this house. $299,000.

The only thing that was suspect was the price—incredibly cheap. "Merrywood," he said repeating the name of the place. He liked the way it sounded, and he also liked the words, "Your family deserves this house."

The advertisement was right. They did deserve it.

"Fantastic!" said Diane after reading the description. "I'd love the pool and the courts. Saturday I have a painting to deliver. Why don't you go see it alone. If you like the place, we will check it out together next weekend."

It was ten at night then when, on impulse, Angus called the realtor.

"Yes. I can show it to you on Saturday, but if you don't mind, I would appreciate your getting here as early as possible," said the realtor, a gentleman named Ronald Croft. Mr. Croft spoke with a soft Southern accent.

Unfortunately Gillespie missed the flight he had counted on and he was more than an hour late, but Croft was understanding. He immediately began to give him a thorough and detailed description of the property.

"I can scarcely believe that this place would not be considerably more expensive," said Gillespie.

"Well, real estate in our part of the country isn't as high as it is farther north."

"But a twelve-room house with substantial acreage around it?"

"The distance from town, I suppose. Perhaps for some it's a bit lonely. Most people want close neighbors. You know what I mean."

"That makes it all the better in my opinion," said Angus. "Neighbors can be a headache. What about the plumbing? Has it been replaced recently?"

"About five years ago."

"Rewired?"

"That was done five years ago, too."

"The drains?"

"They're fine."

"The kitchen?"

"It's been modernized."

"Then loneliness is all people object to about the property?"

"That's all."

"I think it would be the kind of place I would enjoy. After having people constantly coming and going at my New York office and coping with temperamental writers, I can't imagine a peaceful, quiet environment. Can you show me the house?"

Croft looked down at his watch. "It is getting on, isn't it? About fiveish. Later than I thought. Why don't we just look at it in the morning with the sunlight on it. Everything shows up at its worst with evening coming on, doesn't it?"

"I don't find it that important," protested Gillespie. "I'll make allowances for the fact that I'm seeing the house at dusk. Have any ghosts about the place?" he asked, chuckling. "I've heard about you Southerners and your ghost registers!"

"No, the house isn't haunted," Croft replied with a faint, stiff smile. "Although I doubt it would matter much to you if it were, for you don't seem the sort to believe in the supernatural. Do you?" The realtor was not making any move toward leaving his office.

"I would as soon believe in fortune tellers and the like," said Gillespie, somewhat irritably. "This trip has taken me away from manuscripts I should be reading at home, Mr. Croft. May I see the property?" he asked a bit brusquely.

"Of course, of course. I'll take you there myself." He rose and called to the young man across the hall.

"Tim, get me the keys to Merrywood, and tell Bud Farley to bring my car around."

In a few minutes a sleek, black Lincoln was waiting, and they were on their way. It was November and past the season of any fall color. The limbs of bare trees were silhouetted against a bleak, gray sky. Diane would probably have raved about the lines. They passed a field with a hovel probably used by by migrant laborers in season—empty, the windows boarded up, then a stream with a gigantic mill wheel idle against the darkening sky.

"Is it always this quiet and deserted-looking?" asked Gillespie.

"Sometimes more so." Croft looked at his watch. "It's growing dark." Then he looked out the window. "You aren't used to the country, are you?"

"Not really. It will be a change for me."

Gillespie heard the piercing scream of a bird.

"Can you identify bird cries?" he asked his companion.

"No. Just a night bird of some sort, Angus. You don't mind my calling you that, do you? Weird sound, isn't it?"

They had entered a stretch of road that was filled with shadows and gloom under a canopy of intertwined trees. Angus felt a sudden lowering of the temperature even inside the car and closed his coat. This was the entrance to the estate with woods full of large trees on either side of the car, and they were proceeding very slowly.

Looking out the window on his side, he suddenly exclaimed in astonishment. Less than two yards away, and keeping pace with them, two beautiful white Afghan hounds loped beside the car, followed by a man in a brown felt hat and a safari coat. His skin was startlingly pale, and he had a thin, aquiline nose.

"Who the devil is that?"

"Who? I don't see anyone," said Croft, swiveling his head this way and that. "What do you mean?"

"I mean the man walking along beside us with the dogs!" shouted Gillespie.

"I don't see a man," said the realtor, but his face was pale.

"Can't you see them on my side of the car? They are actually keeping pace with us!"

"Of course not, and neither can you," Croft snapped. "It's an hallucination caused by moonlight coming through the branches overhead. I've experienced it more than once." He drove faster.

"Then why don't you see it now?" said Gillespie.

"I'm trying to watch the road. I don't want to miss one of these curves."

Gillespie saw a tree trunk loom up within inches of his window as Croft's white-knuckled hands wrenched the wheel, and they barely missed an oak. At the same time the car seemed to run over some obstacle in the road. Gillespie rolled down the window.

"You've hit something—maybe it's a person. Stop!"

Croft only cursed and slowed a little. Rolling down the window Gillespie strained to see in the darkness, and an icy blast entered the car.

"It's nothing. Just a hole in the road." The realtor accelerated.

"Roll up your window, Mr. Gillespie, before we freeze to death." Gillespie obeyed reluctantly.

Now they were leaving the woods behind them, and moonlight shone on the road ahead. Gillespie looked out his window and started. The man and the beautiful white dogs were there again. He could see the figures vividly and noted the abnormal pallor of the man's face. In order to be sure it was no hallucination Gillespie stared through the window, covering first one eye and then the other. The fellow was slight but well built and ran with the easy grace of an experienced jogger. Gillespie did not believe there was any way man or dogs could keep up with them, even running at top speed. His face began to perspire and he felt an intense horror.

They were approaching an antiquated iron gate and Angus Gillespie knew Mr. Croft would have to get out and leave him alone momentarily while he opened it. He still felt a sense of apprehension. It was a large two-story house with white vine-covered columns.

"This is it," announced the realtor and to Gillespie's surprise he handed him the keys and a flashlight. Croft's face was a pale gray-green.

"Forgive me," said Croft, "but I find myself in need of some medication—"

"I'm sorry. Let's wait a few minutes until you feel better and we can go through the house together. Do you know it well?"

"Yes, yes indeed."

"Then I will wait. Take your medication."

"No, no," protested Croft in a tone bordering on panic. "Go on in. Believe me, I shall follow directly."

Angus looked out and noticed that the runner and dogs were nowhere to be seen.

"Oh, all right. The hallucination or whatever you want to call it seems to have gone." Angus was determined to explore the place that night.

The large old key turned easily in the lock, and he paused to sweep the flashlight beam in a circular motion. He was in an old-fashioned, wainscoted hall with many doors leading off from it, and before him rose an ornately carved staircase. He paused for a moment to admire it. Moonlight streamed through the tall windows, and although the beam of his flashlight was weaker than it might have been, he could see surprisingly well. The clouds skimming across the moon peopled the house with strange shifting shadows, and once he thought he heard stealthy footsteps in the darkness of the back hall.

Was that a white face peering at him? Holding the flashlight with shaking hand he advanced toward it to find it was only a daub of whitewash; he had to smile at himself. Ahead was a door, and as his hand reached for the knob it swung open and something came forth. For a moment he thought he might faint with horror—until he saw that it was only a cat—a lean white cat as frightened as he. But it had created almost as much of a shock as if it had been a ghost.

He gave a sigh of relief and was angry at himself for his nervousness. He knew he should be busily checking the plumbing, the condition of the walls, the wiring, and all the practical features of this house, and he would have had he not seen the figure of the walking man. That and that alone was the cause of his agitated state. He summoned up the courage to go on exploring and cautiously he moved from room to room, halting in suspense every time he heard a noise. The wind was blowing down the chimneys of the house and rattling the window frames.

As he approached the end of a hall on the first floor he saw a dark shape spring forward from the shadows and then move swiftly back. He stood perfectly still, cold perspiration breaking out all over him, his eyes staring into the darkness. What was hiding there?

At last he crept forward toward the shadows, heart pounding; four feet—three—two—he could scarcely breathe. Finally he was there. Nothing sprang out at him. Shining his flashlight beam upon the wall, he saw that what he had feared was only a huge piece of wallpaper torn loose. Each time there was a strong gust of wind it flapped back and forth. The suspense had been so great that he leaned against the wall with relief and laughed until he cried.

Then he heard a noise from somewhere in the basement. Was it his imagination? No. He heard it again. It was probably just the cat knocking something over, but he would go down and investigate. His confidence was returning by leaps and bounds. He decided he liked this house and neither cats nor flapping wallpaper were going to scare him away. Investigating, he found that his conjecture was probably right. An old portrait that had been standing against the wall was face down on the floor.

He conducted a reasonably thorough reconnoiter of the house and was impressed by the arrangement of the rooms. Two baths led off the master bedroom and the two walk-in closets were immense. There was ample space for rooms for the four children, Jennie, Jane, Emma, and Jessica, at one end of the house, and at the other was a study for him and a studio for Diane. They would be able to choose from several possible rooms for their live-in housekeeper.

He opened the front door and Mr. Croft almost fell into his arms.

"I thought, perhaps, I should come to look for you," said Croft. "You've been gone so long."

The space was ideal. It was far enough from town to escape traffic and pollution, yet near enough to make shopping easy. He didn't know why but somehow he felt that this was his house and that the hand of fate was pointing to him as its owner. He had never had quite this feeling before.

"Are you sure the house isn't haunted?" he asked as they drove away from the iron gate.

"Haunted?" Croft gave him a faint smile. "I thought you didn't believe in ghosts."

"I don't. It is just that I have children, and you know how imaginative they are."

"Well, I can't stop their fantasies."

"No, but you can tell me whether other people have imagined anything there."

"Not that I know of."

"Who was the last tenant?"

"A Mr. Eugene Tripp."

"Why did he leave?"

"Who knows. Tired of the area, I guess."

"How long did he stay?"

"Nearly three years."

"Where did he move?"

"I really have no idea. Why do you ask?"

"I would just like to hear about the house from someone who has lived in it. Do you have a forwarding address for him?"

"No. It's been more than two years since he was here."

He debated about calling Diane. He would like to go ahead and take the place. Viewed in the sunlight, it would be just like any other house—mortar and bricks. They did not speak again until they pulled up outside the realtor's office. Gillespie called home and talked at some length to Diane and when he left the phone his face was beaming.

"My wife and I have made up out minds to take it. One year and the option to buy."

This was a typical Gillespie decision—based on emotion and made on the spur of the moment. It had sometimes led him into difficulties. But a month later he and Diane along with the children and their housekeeper were settling in at Merrywood. It was the beginning of December. Almost two months passed before Angus regretted his hasty decision.

Eight-year-old Jennie was home from boarding school for Thanksgiving and the next week. Monday afternoon following the holiday she ran out to the gate to see if her father was in sight. It was about five-thirty and the moon was already high in the sky. Peering over the gate she saw what appeared at a distance to be her father striding toward the house with two of the most beautiful white Afghans she had ever seen.

"Dad!" she cried out. "I can't believe you're bringing us those two dogs."

She raced joyfully toward the figure, and then she stopped short— it was not her father that looked down at her but a stranger with ashen face and enormous, glittering eyes. Jennie fainted. A few minutes later her father came along and found her lying on the ground. From the description the revived child gave him, Gillespie knew it was the man and dogs he had seen on the drive that first day, but he tried to reassure her, saying that the fellow was just a tramp and would probably bother them no more.

A week later Diane's housekeeper gave notice. At first she would not tell them why. Then she said she did not like the house, but when they insisted on her telling them why she finally blurted it out.

"Mrs. Gillespie, I can put up with mice and beetles, but not ghosts. I've had a queer sensation as if water was trickling down my spine ever since I've been here, but I never saw anything until last night. I was in the kitchen getting ready to go to bed—Jane and Emma had already gone up, and I was getting ready to follow them. All of a sudden I heard footsteps, quick and heavy on the gravel outside coming toward the window. It's the boss, I said to myself. Maybe he's forgotten the key and can't get in the front door. I went to the window and was about to open it when I got an awful shock.

"Pressed against the glass, looking in at me, was a face—not the boss's face, not the face of anyone living, but a horrid white thing with a drooping mouth and terrible, glassy eyes—no more expression in them than a pig."

"What do you think it was, Bessie?" asked Diane.

"The face of a corpse, that's what it was. That man had died a terrible death. And on either side of him, standing on their hind legs, were two huge white dogs staring at me. Those dogs were dead too—bad dead. I don't know who did 'em in. Well, they stared at me, all three of them, at least a full minute and it seemed like forever. Then they vanished. Mrs. Gillespie, my heart's not strong, and if I saw them again, it would kill me. That's why I'm leaving."

Diane talked to Angus about it later.

"That tallies with the description of what Jennie saw, yet she said she'd never said a word about it to anyone. Angus, they didn't both imagine it."

He knew now that he should have told his wife of his own experience in the lane and consulted her before taking the house. If she or one of the children should die of fright, he would never forgive himself. There was nothing to do but tell Diane the whole story.

"You mean we not only have the ghost of a man, but of two huge dogs?" Diane said indignantly.

"That's right."

"Then I suggest that you find out a way to get rid of the ghosts, Angus, or we will have to move."

Angus Gillespie drove into town and after some fruitless inquiries about the previous tenant someone referred him to Reese Barnaby, manager of the small bank.

"I'm here because I need to know more about the previous tenant of Merrywood, Mr. Barnaby," said Gillespie bluntly.

The banker's eyes avoided his. "This is a small town—you surely know what I mean. I would like to help you, but I don't want to be placed in the position of gossiping about someone."

"I understand that but frankly my family and I are desperate. That place is haunted, and either we do something about it or we will have to leave."

"Oh, I'd hate to see you people do that," said Barnaby, looking down and clasping his hands nervously. Then he appeared to reach a decision.

"Well, here goes. Some years ago a Mr. Eugene Tripp lived at Merrywood. He never came to town except in the company of one person—his landlord."

"My realtor, Croft?"

"Yes, and according to local gossip they walked about the town arm in arm, visited each other's homes often, and the shopkeepers said they called one another 'Ronny' and 'Gene.'"

"How long did the fellow stay?"

"About three years, and then suddenly people began to say that Gene was gone. No one ever saw him again."

"No address left with the post office?"

"Absolutely none. But here is the strange part of it. A delivery boy returning to town on his bicycle late one afternoon swore he was passed by the pair in Croft's car. The windows were down and he heard loud voices as if they were having a violent argument. Sometime later he overtook the car along that part of the road where the trees overhead are thickest. Croft was just getting in on the driver's side; Tripp was nowhere to be seen nor has anything ever been heard from him since.

"As far as I know no friends or relatives ever came forward to inquire about the fellow. Most of his bills had already been paid—several by Mr. Croft—and no one took the matter up. The boy told his story but Croft only laughed at it saying it, was a lie and that he had been in another part of the state looking at property that day and didn't get back to town until almost midnight. He maintained that all he knew was Tripp had expressed his intention of leaving before his lease expired, so he had claimed the furniture in lieu of the rent due him."

"Did the matter drop there?" asked Gillespie.

"Yes and no. Within a few weeks there were rumors that Tripp's ghost had been seen at the place you say you saw it on the road. Many people have seen it—I have myself for that matter."

"Has anyone tried to speak to it?"

"Yes—and it vanished at once."

"Any theory about it?"

"I guess my theory is about the same as everyone else's, but loose talk is dangerous."

"Did Mr. Tripp have any dogs?"

"Yes. Two beautiful white Afghan hounds. The man was crazy about those dogs, and for some reason his fussing over them angered Croft. Everyone noticed it. "

"I think I'm going to try to lay those ghosts."

"Do you want me to come with you?"

"No. I would rather be alone."

Later Gillespie was to wish he had taken Barnaby up on his offer. He had refused it in a well-lighted room with the sounds of the employees and clients of the bank just outside the office door. Half an hour later as he was approaching the darkest part of the road to the old house, he would have been delighted to have companionship.

He was almost at the same spot where he had seen the man and dogs the first time when he saw them again. Before he knew it they were at his side and they kept up with the car. His window was down and twice he tried to speak to the man but found himself too horrified to utter a word. Then he averted his eyes as if his refusal to look would make the apparitions disappear, but turning his head again, he saw they were still there, as if stalking him. To his relief, when he reached Merrywood they dashed past.

Gillespie, much ashamed of his lack of courage, told Diane, and she insisted on accompanying him the following afternoon to the place where the ghosts appeared. They had not been there over a few minutes when their youngest daughter, Jessica, came running up to them with a telegram. Diane read it and was about to speak to her husband, but the words never left her lips. She lifted a hand and pointed at something. Gillespie and Jessica turned to look.

Standing and staring at them was the slight, spare figure of a young man with a white face and dull, lifeless eyes. He was dressed in expensive but casual walking clothes. Beside him were the Afghan hounds. Angus and his wife started to speak but could not.

Jessica seemed to feel no such fear.

"Who are you?" she said walking up to the figure. "You must feel very ill to look so pale. Tell me your name."

The man made no reply. He turned away and slowly glided up to a huge oak. Then, pointing with the index finger of his right hand at the tree, he appeared to sink into the earth and vanish. The Gillespies walked over to the tree and on examining it found that it was hollow. Inside it were three skeletons—a human being and two dogs. Recovering themselves enough to summon the police, the Gillespies told them the story of what had happened and pointed out the tree with its ghastly secret. Fragments of clothing were still clinging to the human remains. According to the medical examiner's later report, it was the skeleton of a young woman. The skull had received a violent blow, undoubtedly causing the death. Gillespie also related his first visit to see the house, the appearance of the ghosts, and Croft's peculiar behavior.

Ronald Croft was arrested on suspicion of murder. He confessed and in his confession said that his wife was so beautiful he was afraid of losing her to another man, thus he had forced her to dress in men's clothing. The next morning when the guard brought breakfast he found Croft hanging by his belt from the roof of his cell. The realtor had left a brief note.

She was my wife—I loved her. She became a dog worshiper, loving the dogs more than me. I couldn't bear it. I killed her and her dogs.

It was a sad and ugly story. But the ghosts were no more, Angus bought his daughter two beautiful Afghan hounds, and the Gillespie family lived on happily at Merrywood for many years.

Captain Kidd's Farewell

SITTING ON THE FLOOR, paws folded in front of him, Captain waited while his nine-year-old mistress prepared for bed. After brushing her long strawberry blonde hair, Jennifer reached over, gathered up the large cat, and buried her face in the silky, two-inch-long black and white fur. He purred contentedly.

"Now it's your turn," said Jennifer, selecting a smaller brush from the bedside table. The cat began to squirm.

"Stop that, Captain! Let me brush you. You're going to get hairballs if you don't behave." She held him firmly by his collar. A resigned Captain ceased struggling.

"Now you're all shiny and beautiful."

Jennifer snuggled down under the covers, and the cat lay back against her leg, using it to brace himself as he performed his nightly ablutions. She could feel him move as he bathed, first one part of his body and then another, until he finished the nightly ritual by licking the tufts of fur between the pads of each paw. Jennifer was sound asleep by the time Captain had bathed to his satisfaction, and rested his furry chin upon her bare ankle.

When she woke up it was a warm June morning, and she could hear the sounds of pots and pans and water running in the kitchen. Sunlight was streaming through the window, and she lay there for a few minutes, her heart quickening with anticipation. This was the day her mother would be driving her up to spend a week with her grandmother at Hendersonville. She thought about "Maw-maw's" cool house in the shadow of the North Carolina mountains.

She felt Captain place a soft paw delicately on the side of her face, and the message was clear. He was letting her know he was hungry and it was time to get up. Her bedroom was a dainty and cheerful lavender, one end papered with flowers, a suitable bower for the head of her maple bed. She threw back the lavender quilt.

"Jennifer, Jennifer, are you up?" called her mother. "Breakfast is almost ready, and we want to leave by nine-thirty."

Her father was sitting at the table drinking his coffee and reading the paper. Her mother had just put the bacon on paper towels to drain, and begun scrambling eggs when she turned to spot Captain crawling up into the top drawer below the countertop.

"Uh-oh! Honey, get Captain."

Thirteen-year-old Captain's high-jumping days were over, but he had become an adept drawer opener, crawling into one above the other to reach the counter. Jennifer lifted him from the second drawer before he reached his objective—the bacon.

"It's no accident that cat was named after a pirate," her mother said, smiling.

"Dad, are you really descended from the pirate, Captain Kidd?" Jennifer asked.

"Yes. I keep my cutlass and treasure in the attic for safekeeping," said her father.

"We think his ancestors are descended from William Kidd's brother," explained her mother. "Either Thomas, or a close relative."

"And that's why you named our cat Captain, Dad?"

"Yes."

"Well, he's sweet anyway, and I love him."

"I think he knows that. It's you he always sleeps with," said her dad. "I remember when you were only four years old and he came in with a badly hurt paw—so bad we had to take him to the vet the next morning. He went straight up to your bed, honey. We finally had to take him out of the bed and it wasn't easy, but your mother and I were afraid you would roll over on him in the night."

"That really could have hurt him."

"Yes, and not understanding, he might have bitten you." Jennifer's father, Richard Kidd, was a staff sergeant in the Air National Guard on weekends and a civil employee during the week.

Her mother, Judy Kidd, worked almost every weekend as communications director for the Gastonia police station and she was thrilled to have a day off at Maw-maw's. Her job was 911 duty and everything seemed to happen on the weekends. "You have to be on your toes," she would say. "It may be an accident on I-85 or it could be a dangerous domestic situation involving drinking."

Jennifer gathered up her sweater, a paper sack full of mint plants for her grandmother, and her suitcase. She got in the car with her mother. Fifty miles from home, halfway to Hendersonville, Jennifer remembered she had not told Captain goodbye.

"You'll see him in a week, and when I get back I'll give him a big hug for you," said her mother.

A few miles from the resort town of Hendersonville Jennifer could see the mountains, and that meant they were not far from her grandmother's comfortable, sprawling, split-level home. Jennifer was an independent child, and it made her feel very grown-up to be allowed to spend a week alone with her grandmother. She had been making these visits for several years, and had her very own bedroom at Maw-maw's.

Maw-maw, a tiny, vivacious Latin woman, gave Jennifer a warm hug when they arrived, and everyone sat down to enjoy lunch. Then came goodbye kisses, and Jennifer's parents headed back to Gastonia.

At home that evening, after Richard and Judy enjoyed a quiet dinner, Richard and Captain began to wrestle. Captain started the play session by making a fierce sham attack on Richard's ankle. After a half-hour of pouncing and dodging, Captain began bumping his head against the screen to indicate he wanted to go out. Richard opened the door and retired for the evening.

Earlier that same day Jennifer and her grandmother went to the mall, and after supper they turned on the television, but Jennifer was too sleepy to watch. She said she would read in bed but when her grandmother looked in on her around nine o'clock, she was sound asleep.

In the middle of the night Jennifer suddenly woke up. Something had landed on her bed—*plop!* She knew that it was Captain and was about to go back to sleep—until all at once, she realized with a shock that she was not at home, she was at her grandmother's, and there was no Captain here to leap upon her bed. Now she was truly frightened. She slipped across the hall to her grandmother's room.

"Maw-maw. Maw-maw! Wake up. Please. Captain jumped on my bed and it scared me."

"Captain? Honey, Captain's at home."

"No. He jumped on my bed right here. I felt it shake the foot of the bed just like it does at home."

"You were probably dreaming about him."

"No. I wasn't dreaming." Jennifer was trembling. "May I get in bed with you?"

"Of course."

But Jennifer did not go back to sleep for a long time.

The next morning was June 20, Father's Day, and her grandmother suggested she call home and wish her dad a happy Father's Day.

"I'll do it right away, and Maw-maw, I want to tell him about Captain's jumping on my bed last night."

When she told her father how she had been awakened in the night, he said very little and he did not assure her it had been a dream as her grandmother had done. She was surprised to see his blue Chevrolet there when she and her grandmother pulled up in the drive after church. Instead of giving her the big smile she expected his face was solemn as he hugged her.

"Jennifer, honey. I have something to tell you, and I thought it would be better if I drove up and we talked about it."

"What is it, Daddy?"

"This morning Captain was not at the back door. We called him and he didn't come, so your mother and I went out searching the neighborhood for him. We finally found him under one of our own holly bushes near the house. He was curled up like he was taking a nap."

"And was he, Daddy?"

"No, honey, he was dead. He hadn't been in a fight, and he didn't have a mark on him. I think he had gone peacefully off to sleep and just never woke up."

"Oh! Daddy!" There was a flood of tears as Jennifer's father held her in fast his arms.

"But he was here just last night ...."

"What in the world do you mean?"

And then, between sobs, she told her father how she had been awakened by Captain suddenly landing upon her bed in the middle of the night and how it had startled her so that she had to go in and sleep with her grandmother the rest of the night.

"Suppose he was out there sick, Daddy, or needed help?"

"I don't think there was anything we could do, honey. Captain played with me the night before and was just fine, but he was thirteen years old, and that's getting on for a cat. I suppose it was just time for him to go."

"But why did I feel him leap on my bed? I knew right away it was him!" she cried.

"I think he came to tell you goodbye."

"Do you really, Daddy?"

"Yes, I do. I think Captain wanted to let you know he loved you very much, Jennifer."

HORSE GHOSTS

The Ghost at Wickersham Hall

"DO VISIT US AT EASTER," wrote Marcus to his old friend, Dugald MacRae. "I am sure this country estate will interest you. It is haunted."

Dugald wanted to go, although he suspected that his old friend invented the part about Wickersham Hall being haunted. Marcus knew, after all, that Dugald had a longstanding interest in the supernatural.

When Dugald's train left London's Waterloo Station on Good Friday, the weather was growing worse by the hour—a storm was on the way. When he arrived at Wickersham Station he was surprised to find a black carriage with closed curtains awaiting him. Dugald mounted the sideboard of the somber brougham and stepped into its musty interior, amused by this reminder of his friend's eccentricities.

Carriages were a rarity in this day, but Marcus Span was never one to use an automobile when a horse-drawn vehicle would do instead! Jolting along the rutted country road to Wickersham Hall in the brougham, he began to wonder about the letter. Could Marcus have been serious about the haunting?

As Dugald passed through the gates of the estate, he was impressed with the grounds. Was it beauty? Not in the accepted sense; rather, it was a picture of magnificent desolation. The withered, weed-choked grass, the unkempt hedges, and the decayed trees were a perfect setting for the house that rose bleak and massive before him. The day was raw and cold but the atmosphere grew positively frigid as he entered the grounds. A dreariness hung over Wickersham. Dugald looked at his watch. It was four-thirty and the light was fading fast.

As the carriage rolled on through the park, Dugald felt a sudden sense of uneasiness. The sensation was uncommonly strong, but as the carriage drew nearer to the house this feeling gradually faded. He chastised himself for heeding his overactive imagination; all would be forgotten after a brandy before the fire.

An elaborate knocker clanked beneath Dugald's hand, and Marcus himself welcomed him warmly. Although the entrance hall was elegant, the dark oak paneling produced an air of gloom. This house was certainly the ideal setting for a ghost, but strangely enough Dugald felt a lot more comfortable than he had during the drive from the gate to the mansion.

Marcus immediately asked, "Did you experience any unusual sensations as you entered the house?" He hung Dugald's warm cashmere overcoat in a closet under the stairs.

"I think so," replied Dugald, now thinking his feelings foolish, perhaps more induced by the depressing old vehicle, the unkempt look of the grounds, and his friend's warning.

"Most people do."

"Has anyone ever seen anything?"

"Not so far as I know, but the noises we hear around the house are becoming more frequent."

"Noises?"

"I would prefer not to describe them, Dugald. I don't want to bias you."

At that moment his wife, Jennifer, entered the hall and graciously extended both hands to him. She was about thirty-five with chestnut colored hair. Her lovely coloring was like an autumn leaf. Jennifer loved sports and her graceful, lithe figure was evidence.

"Do join us," said she and led the way.

A large house party was going on in the library overlooking the garden. There was a game of cards in progress, a woman playing Debussy at the piano, and a young couple standing near the windows deep in private conversation. After introductions, the three sat before the fire and reminisced over a brandy. Nothing more was said about ghosts.

Dugald went to bed thinking that he would listen for noises, but he was tired and the long, cold ride followed by brandy and the warmth of the room had made him excessively sleepy. He did not wake until after eight o'clock the next morning.

At breakfast Dugald found everyone cheerful and friendly, and he was in time to hear Marcus announce that there was to be a masked ball that evening. The others applauded, for the Spans were well known for original parties, but inwardly Dugald groaned. He despised dressing in costume and wouldn't have been caught dead in kilts, but he decided he must do his best to appear to enjoy it. He also remembered that Marcus celebrated an old-fashioned English Easter custom—the exchange of gifts, so after lunch, he borrowed Jennifer's car and headed for a nearby town to shop.

By the time he was driving back to the estate it was nearing five o'clock, and massive, dark clouds were rolling across the horizon. There was still enough light left to explore the grounds, though, so Dugald decided to have a look around.

He had no sooner entered a wooded area than he was aware of the same presence he had felt the afternoon before on his arrival. His uneasiness returned. The presence was less noticeable in some places then others, and strangely enough, it seemed to suggest a path. He made himself follow it. Eventually he came to a stop in front of a rock wall, and through the brush, which was still without leaves, gaped a dark, irregular opening. It was the mouth of a large cavern, and from its roof hung numerous stalactites.

As Dugald entered the cave, he noticed a strange musky scent in the air. He followed the scent until it became so pungent he thought he must have reached its origin. He could make out nothing but jagged walls and blackness until suddenly, deep in the cavern depths, a faint glow of crimson light appeared. A light which grew and grew and grew. Gradually and horribly the light split into two enormous eyes that stared out menacingly. The presence he had felt upon his arrival at Wickersham Hall was now only a few feet away from him.

Dugald struggled to recover his self-possession. He tried to tell himself that this could be an extraordinary discovery—but it was no use. As the eyes advanced they became more fierce, hostile, and menacing. He tried to open his mouth and shout for help but it was like a nightmare—no sound came, and his lungs felt as if they would burst with tension. The musky odor was overpowering. The eyes rushed toward Dugald out of the darkness, and for the first time in his life he felt helpless, as if in the grip of some supernatural power. Then he felt the full force of the attack. The creature bit and kicked him mercilessly until he lost consciousness. Coming to and finding himself alone, he stumbled out of the cave.

He reached the house after dark, greeted an anxious Marcus and Jennifer, and related his experience.

"I'm ashamed to say that when those eyes were close upon me, I couldn't seem to defend myself. I must be a mass of bruises."

"Dugald, there isn't a mark on you."

"I don't believe it!" Dugald went to the mirror over the fireplace and examined his head and neck incredulously, for Marcus was right.

"That cave is the most haunted spot on the grounds, and it's no place to go after dark," said Marcus Span, his face white. "Promise me that you won't do it again."

"At this moment I'm tempted to promise, but I had better not, Marcus. I will want to go back. You knew when you invited me that I couldn't resist a mystery."

"Dugald, I wouldn't go to that cave alone myself," confessed his host, "and I hope you won't either." There was real concern in his face. "I've been there several times at night with a group of friends, and we have experienced some horrifying sensations."

"Sensations are mild compared to what I've just been through," said Dugald, "marks or not." He stared at his face in the hall mirror and saw a tall, bearded man with blue eyes that usually looked out on life with considerable humor. At the moment they were clouded with shock. He opened his shirt to check his body.

"Not a mark on me. I can't believe this!"

"It must be some sort of devil," said Jennifer.

"You may want to have that cave filled in or blasted," suggested Dugald.

"An excellent idea," agreed Marcus.

"But not until I finish my investigation," Dugald warned. His host frowned with anxiety, and his lips closed, forming a thin line.

That night Dugald woke, and when he looked at his watch it was one o'clock. He had the strongest feeling that someone or something was prowling outside his windows. At last, yielding to his impulse to see, he rose. There was a full moon, and beneath his window, he saw the dark blurred outline of some immense creature. He heard the movements, the sound of branches breaking in the shrubbery, and he stared down toward the noise. As he did huge, glowing eyes, red and satanical, turned toward him. His heart thudded as if it would burst his breast. He stood spellbound until somewhere close at hand a dog barked and the eyes vanished.

It was daybreak before Dugald was able to get back to sleep. He was sure he had only just dozed off when he was awakened by bangings on doors, laughter and everyone exchanging Easter greetings. He would like to have slept all morning but the uneasy feeling caused by his night visitor still lingered, and he decided to go to church with the hope of dispelling the fear that afflicted him. But although he punctiliously repeated the responses in the prayer book, this morning the routine of the liturgy did not provide its usual comfort.

What was the strange creature with the glowing eyes? Why had it been under his window last night? Was his interest in the supernatural attracting it?

There had been no time to share his experience of the night before because of the guests, and he had decided not to. Marcus had mentioned hearing noises in the house, but that was all. Was the vision he saw out the window a remnant of his encounter at the cave the previous evening? Had his imagination recreated the fearful, glowing eyes? He kept his peace.

Later that day, after luncheon, Marcus asked, "What would you think of a drive this afternoon? There's a charming, picturesque village not many miles from here." Dugald was delighted.

They set out about one-thirty—not in an automobile but in the carriage, as he might have expected—and arrived at three o'clock. Rolling along winding streets, few of them paved, passing quaint houses and shops with thatched roofs, they visited a small, beautifully designed cathedral—the focal point of the village. Then they explored the village in a leisurely fashion. Though it was Sunday and none of the shops were open, they stared in the windows. Marcus began upon a subject that always irritated Dugald.

"It surprises me that you haven't considered settling down and beginning a family. Surely your investigations of the supernatural are not so intensive as to take the place of home and hearth?"

"I consider it at times, but I haven't been fortunate enough to meet someone like Jennifer," parried Dugald. "Meanwhile, I have a comfortable little flat in London, and no one is upset if I do not return when expected from one of my business trips."

"You make it sound ideal."

"It is not, but it beats the eternal tug of war some men have with wives who resent the unpredictable demands of work."

"Dugald!" he exclaimed, "with the fortune your father left, you will never have to work, while even those of us who consider ourselves among the privileged have the duties of an estate."

"True."

"Do you really consider your investigations 'business'?"

"I don't think being a barrister, a baker, or a candlestick maker is the only criterion for business," Dugald said, bristling.

"Of course, you're right," said Marcus hastily, and they were quiet for awhile.

"If you solve our situation, there is no need to cut your visit short. I know you become restless if you are not working on some mystery but you come to the country so seldom."

Dugald's expression softened. Their friendship dated back over a decade, and he never stayed irritated with Marcus for long.

They soon decided it was time to head for Wickersham Hall. The horse trotting briskly, they were climbing a hill almost within sight of home when a startling change occurred. The temperature dropped considerably.

"Brrrr. What's going on here!" exclaimed Dugald, turning up his coat collar. As he spoke their horse suddenly shied, and the carriage lurched precariously.

"Does she do this often?"

"Only when we're on this road this time of day," came the tight-lipped reply. "Sit tight and keep your eyes open, Dugald."

They were now traveling through the kind of desolate country that reminded him of his surroundings on his first ride to Wickersham—barren hills, areas of tangled wilderness, and somber valleys. As they passed a large quarry filled with water, from which branches and other debris protruded, he thought he saw something large and white—bright white—rising from its depths. But his glimpse of it was fleeting because their horse was now pulling the carriage at a lightning pace down a long slope. The cold was numbing. Neither man spoke. The swift, steady clap of the horse's hoofs on the hard road was hypnotic.

They were halfway down the hill when, from the direction of the quarry behind them, Dugald heard a deafening, reverberating neigh. Startled, he looked back to see a magnificent stallion standing on the crest of the hill above them, outlined against the dusk. The animal was a shining, luminous white and gigantic. Their mare was fully aware of the stallion's presence. Their carriage hurtled forward. If his hands had not been clutching the side after his friend's warning to "sit tight," he would have been thrown.

They were now moving even faster, the mare frantic with terror. Dugald looked back. The white stallion was not thirty yards behind them. Even in the failing light of dusk, he could see the beast clearly for a glow emanated from its body—broad, heavily muscled breast, steaming flanks and long, graceful legs with shoeless, shining hoofs. Fearful as he was, he could not help but admire the sight. Its back was arched and powerful, its head was magnificent with its broad, massive forehead and waving forelock, its strides monstrous, its mane rippling in the wind. He could see the distended nostrils and the open, foaming mouth revealing huge, glistening teeth. On and on it came.

And then it was upon him. There was an icy blast at his neck, and a great hiss from the animal's nostrils. Its breath, close to his face, drained all resistance away, and as he felt the teeth of the gigantic horse crunching down upon his neck he lost consciousness.

When Dugald came to, he found himself sitting with his back to the wall in the library, Jennifer pouring brandy generously down his throat.

"As the mare left the road to take the drive that led up to Wickersham, she took it too sharply, and the carriage overturned," she explained. "Marcus is dreadfully sorry and sends his apologies. You and he were thrown clear of it, but he is in bed for I'm afraid he has injured his shoulder rather badly. You gave me quite a scare when you didn't come around for so long."

"How did I get in the library?" Dugald asked, looking around him.

"We brought you in here because there was a fire."

"Where is Marcus?"

"He's in bed in his room, and the doctor will be here soon."

"Did Marcus see it?"

"See what?"

"The white horse," said Dugald a trifle impatiently.

"I don't know. You can talk to him tomorrow."

"Tomorrow! Not now?"

"No. Neither of you are up to it," she said firmly, as one of the servants brought in a hot, damp towel.

"Your neck is all red and there are welts upon it. You must have scraped it against the side of the carriage."

"It wasn't that at all," he began heatedly. "It was—"

"Please ... be still," said Jennifer soothingly wrapping the towel around his neck. "Don't try to talk now. We won't know what other injuries you have until the doctor checks you."

"I want to get up and see Marcus," he protested, and tried to rise, but his legs were wobbly beneath him and he sank back. The room was slipping out of focus and he slept, rousing briefly while the doctor checked him, then swallowing a sedative and going back to sleep.

The following morning Dugald awoke to find himself bruised and sore, but with no broken bones. When he appeared for breakfast, Jennifer had already finished. She sat sipping a cup of mint tea.

"You were fortunate not to be injured, Dugald. Marcus is feeling better this morning, but the doctor said he has a broken rib."

"That's a shame. Has he said anything about the horse, Jennifer?"

"Oh, the mare is not injured. Now if you'll excuse me for a few minutes—"

"Of course."

He looked at her curiously, realizing she had thought he meant the horse pulling the carriage. Marcus must not have wanted her to know what had spooked his mare and caused the accident. Jennifer went out to the garden and returned in a short while with a basket full of beautiful spring daffodils. She arranged them deftly in a vase.

"Now. Shall we go in and see Marcus?"

Dugald followed her into a large, sunny bedroom on the main floor and pulled up a chair beside the carved four-poster mahogany bed.

"Terribly sorry about that rib, Marcus. I know it must hurt like the devil. Here, let me help you."

He reached for the cup that Marcus was painfully trying to replace on the table beside his bed and did it for him. Then he asked the question he had wanted to ask since he first regained consciousness.

"What did you think of that monstrous white horse chasing us?"

"I saw your face, and I knew you must be seeing something awful, but I couldn't see it."

"You couldn't!"

"No. But I don't doubt for a minute that it was there; I heard it coming up behind us, and Dugald, I felt its presence. Bloody frightening! But tell me everything you saw."

When his friend finished he said bluntly, "This ability you have to see such things is more of a curse than a blessing. I don't envy you."

"You were right all along, then, Marcus," said his wife in surprise and he nodded. "You have said since the beginning that the ghost was a horse."

"I have long suspected it. I attribute its hauntings to the remains of early horses I found in that cave a few months back. I thought they might have come from the days of William the Conqueror in 1066 or sometime during the next century or so when the English started breeding oversize horses for battle. We may never know. But those horses, bred to carry a man in armor, were immense—six feet high and weighing more than a ton. They would dwarf a modern-day horse! We kept one of the skeletons and presented the others to a museum. The bones of many more horses are probably resting at the same spot."

"You are probably right," said Dugald. "But take my advice, Marcus, and let them rest. Bury the bones you have already unearthed. If you go on excavating and keeping the bones, the disturbances are likely to increase, and the hauntings may become more severe."

When Dugald returned to London he found a letter awaiting him.

Dear Dugald,
    Thank you for advising us on our situation here. I have had the bones of the one horse re-interred and the excavation filled in. As far as we can tell the hauntings have ceased.
    My shoulder continues to remind me of our adventure! Jennifer and I look forward to your company on a future visit.
                                        Sincerely,
                                        Marcus

Dugald touched the red scrape on the side of his neck gingerly as he looked in his shaving mirror. And as he did he felt an icy blast of air from the open window behind him. Once more he beheld in his mind's eye a mammoth white stallion, saw again the fiery eyes and the gaping mouth. Then, trailing a luminous cloud of white mist, the steed from the past was gone.

The Ponies of Tule Canyon

WHEN THE ROUNDTREE FAMILY stopped at the Texas Panhandle town of Tulia, it was a warm September day in 1936. They were on their way back east from New Mexico, and decided to do some shopping. Spencer Roundtree pulled his new robin's egg blue Ford convertible up in front of the town's largest general store. Inside his wife and son began chatting with a friendly rancher and his granddaughter—a meeting that would lead to an unforgettable night.

Tall, sturdily built with a shock of white hair and a deeply tanned face, S.M. Rodgers seldom met a stranger. During the next half hour he took a genuine liking to the Roundtrees and invited the whole family to be his guests for the night at the Rodgers ranch.

"You oughta take him up on it," urged Mort Hamer, who owned the store. "Old Oklahoma there knows some good stories about the history of this part of Texas. He used to ride in the cavalry out here."

Rodgers smiled at this. Even now, at the age of 83, he was still punching cattle.

"Tell them the one about the horses."

"To me that's an ugly story," said Rodgers. "I wish we could forget it."

"The supernatural part is interesting."

"And I don't believe a bit of it."

"Well, you'll tell them anyway, Oklahoma. I know you."

"You folks call me Oklahoma, too," Rodgers said jovially. "That's what everyone else does. Just follow Patricia and me to the house." His ranch was about fourteen miles away at the mouth of Tule canyon. With a boy's enthusiasm he waved his ten-gallon hat toward the road and they followed.

Staring in dismay at the gray cloud of dust in the wake of the Rodgers truck, Roundtree hung back a bit in the open convertible just to be able to see. But Spencer felt a sense of adventure as he followed

47

this lively octogenarian. They were carried along by the old man's ebullience and that sense of expectancy that seems to hang in the air during a beautiful Texas September day. Sixteen-year-old Alan was riding up ahead in the black Ford truck with Oklahoma and his granddaughter, Patricia, and she began to relate the history of the Texas canyon area.

"All this land was once inhabited by the Kiowa and Comanche Indians," she said gesturing grandly. "They called it *Comancheria.*"

"Comancheria ... I like the sound of it."

"I like it too, but you wouldn't have liked the Comanches," said Patricia, rolling her eyes in mock fear. "They were awesome fighters."

"Comanches and Kiowas roamed these plains for miles most of the year fighting enemies, hunting and raiding other tribes for horses. After the fall hunt when they had lots of buffalo meat they would go down the steep, narrow trails into the canyons and camp there all winter," said Patricia. "The high walls provided a refuge from their enemies and also from wind and harsh cold."

"It's rugged country," said Alan.

"My grandfather says they used to call it the Great American Desert. Probably looks pretty desolate to you, but I love it!"

Alan had been bored by history in school, but never had it been taught to him by such a pretty professor. He stared at the vivacious, red-haired girl. Her silver spurs were worn loose, California style, chain under the instep of her small boots. Listening to her talk and gazing at the plains all around him, Indian attacks seemed much more real than they did back east.

Mrs. Rodgers, a plump woman with curly white hair and eyes still bright as jet, prepared supper—beef, potatoes, sourdough bread, sliced tomatoes and corn on the cob. They ate heartily.

Later, on the front porch, the Roundtrees began to ask questions.

"The canyons we passed—those walls were so beautiful, all pinkish gold and orange. Do they have names?" asked Mrs. Roundtree.

"Most of them do. That was the canyon of the Tule with that magnificent basin at its western end. The basin has multicolored walls along the banks of the Tule."

"You must know a great deal about the history out here," said Spencer Roundtree.

His host nodded proudly. "I came out here in 1897 with my wife and eight of my ten children in a covered wagon. Lived on this land ever since," said Oklahoma, and he launched into vivid tales from long ago. His guests from back east began to visualize the vastness of the Indian's land of Comancheria, the early days of the Texas Panhandle, and the arrival of horses and cattle.

"First came Coronado in 1540, his men dressed in their glittering finery riding on the backs of a thousand Spanish horses. Behind the procession came a noisy, bellowing herd of five hundred cattle with a cloud of dust hovering over it. Most of the cattle had been raised on Mexican ranches to supply meat for the conquistadores' entourage.

"Three centuries later, when the first English speaking colonists reached Texas, they found wild cattle and wild horses, mostly Spanish, in the southern and eastern areas. About the time I arrived cattle raisers from the British Isles were beginning to import the great breeds which our cattle today are descended from."

"What about buffalo?" asked Alan Roundtree.

"They were everywhere."

"And the Indians survived on the buffalo," said Mrs. Rodgers as she sat down in a rocker on the porch.

"That's true," Oklahoma agreed. "The Indians lived on the meat, clothed themselves with buffalo skins and made tepees of the hide.

"But back to horses, Roundtree, they'd been escaping from the Spanish herds for a hundred and thirty years. In those days there was a solid turf of green grass as far as the eye could see for the horses to graze on and enough water to survive. Of course, the Indians learned to ride, hunt buffalo and make war on horseback. They stole horses from the ranchers but didn't bother the cattle—had no use for cattle because they liked buffalo meat best.

"Ranching the way it was being done out here was new to settlers from back east, but they soon picked up Spanish ways. They started wearing leather chaps and broad-brimmed hats, learned how to handle a bucking horse, use a lasso, ride in a saddle that had a horn for their rope and use the big spurs of the Mexicans. The cowboys were a blend of Mexican, Spanish, and American.

"Well, the great cattle towns are history now—Abilene, Dodge City, Wichita. They came to life with the railroads and a brilliant young entrepreneur named Joe McCoy. Confident, colorful, everybody knew him by his black slouch hat, goatee and heavy boots. It was McCoy who opened Abilene to the Texas longhorn trade.

"Ever heard of the Chisholm Trail?" he continued. Mr. Roundtree nodded.

"You wouldn't believe how it started. Early drovers and cowboys on their way from Fort Worth toward the Cimarron River in Oklahoma saw something they never expected to see. In the middle of nowhere— when they hadn't met a soul for days—they came across a wide swath on the prairie where the grass was beaten down by iron wheel tracks. Tracks from wagons traveling north-south. They learned later that they had been made by an Indian trader named Chisholm.

The tracks didn't go far, just over a hundred and fifty miles, but soon everybody was calling the whole thing the 'Chisholm Trail'."

"I've heard of it all my life—like the Santa Fe and the Oregon Trail," said Mr. Roundtree thoughtfully. "And it all started from a stretch of wheel tracks only a hundred and fifty miles long."

"That's right. Most Texans just called it 'The Trail,'" said Oklahoma. It was a long, hard trek with little water for cattle, harsh weather and Indian attacks, "but trail bosses and cowboys all followed it dreaming of women, whiskey and the jingle of hard money in their pockets. The first sign those trail-weary longhorns and drovers had that they were nearing one of the great cattle towns was its odor. It was much more pungent than that of their own herd—people couldn't have stood it today—but they were too happy to notice. They could hardly wait to get to noisy, dusty Abilene with the new Drovers Cottage hotel sitting like a palace among the rest of the log buildings."

Alan was showing real interest. "What about Dodge City and Bat Masterson, Mr. Rodgers?"

"Alan, most people don't know it, but the famous lawman didn't kill anyone in or around Dodge, according to the cattle town newspaper. His brother, George, tended bar in a dance house, and Bat just hung out there to keep things orderly."

The boy stared down at the gnarled hands, hands that had held the reins of a covered wagon! He regarded Rodgers reverently. He had never met a real pioneer—a man who had been alive at the same time as "Wild Bill" Hickok and Wyatt Earp. He could almost see the way it looked in those days.

"There's a story about the very place this ranch is on, isn't there?" asked the boy.

"I know you don't like to tell that one, and you always claim that the ghost part of it is just superstition, but why don't you?" said Mrs. Rodgers to her husband.

"A ghost story?" Alan's interest quickened.

"Just legend. I don't take much stock in it myself."

"Tell us the story anyway, Oklahoma," urged Alan's father. He, too, was impressed by the old man.

"It's too late to tell that one tonight." Rodgers grimaced as if in distaste and shook his head.

"Please, Grandfather," begged Patricia, and he gave in.

"Well, all right. There'd been Indian attacks along the Kansas and Texas frontiers—mostly renegades who had fled the reservations. General C.C. Augur, who was commander of the Department of Texas, determined he would put a stop to it and punish the Indians by mounting a five-pronged offensive to drive them back. The Army had been skirmishing with them to the northeast along the Canadian and Red River and here in the Panhandle.

"One of the commanding officers under Augur was a Colonel Ranald S. Mackenzie. It was his mission to close the lower jaw of the vise on the Indian escapees. His orders from General Auger were, 'Take such measures against them as will, in your judgment, soonest accomplish the purpose.'

"Mackenzie organized an expedition of about 600 men at Fort Concho, where San Angelo is today, and they marched to Freshwater Fork on the Brazos River. Camping there, he sent out 32 scouts— Seminoles, Negroes, Lipan, Tonkawa Indians and white men. They searched unsuccessfully for days until finally the Seminoles reported finding three trails that seemed worth following.

"Starting in the direction of Tule Canyon, the trails grew warmer and the troopers began to clash with small parties of Indians."

"We saw part of Tule Canyon on our way here to the house," said Roundtree.

"That's right. But to get on with my story—it was sundown on the 25th of September in 1871, and the men had dismounted to camp when one of the scouts rode in, reporting he had located the Indians.

"He jumped down from his horse all excited, saying, 'They're east of the Tule. Fresh trails are all over the place.' The troopers went after them.

"By the next night they were so close to the main body of Indians that the troopers slept with their boots on, keeping their weapons within easy reach. Mackenzie knew the target would be his horses, so he posted pickets around the camp every fifteen feet and sleeping parties of a dozen or more men stayed inside the herd.

"About ten-fifteen that night, the alarm sounded. One hundred and fifty Indians charged the camp, but after about thirty minutes of fighting they withdrew. From then on everything was quiet until almost daylight. The men were asleep when suddenly at least three hundred Indians appeared on a ridge overlooking the camp and began to fire. One of the companies charged, returning the fusillade of bullets, and after a time the Indians disappeared. That ended the fighting here at the canyon. The troopers broke camp next afternoon.

"This led the Indians to believe that any danger from them was over, but after dark Mackenzie ordered a surprise move. Turning northwest he led his troops across the plains toward Palo Duro. On the way his scouts found a wide trail. They followed it, lost it, then found it again. Reaching the edge of Palo Duro Canyon, the scouts looked down with astonishment. Far below them they saw hundreds of horses grazing, and Indian tepees covering the canyon floor stretched for two or three miles—Kiowas, Comanches, Cheyennes. Hating life on the reservation, they had fled to the canyon. It had long been a traditional winter shelter with good grazing, tall trees and the steep walls securing it from attack.

"Since Mackenzie's men had marched away before turning north, the Indians thought that the troopers were abandoning pursuit. They hadn't even stationed sentries along the bluff overlooking the canyon. At first no trail could be found leading down into the canyon, but finally the troopers found a narrow, zigzag path that descended from about nine hundred feet above the canyon floor. They would have to descend single file leading their horses—perhaps into an ambush. At daybreak they mounted and started out, horses slipping and stumbling as they made their way carefully down the steep trail to the canyon floor.

"When they reached it the Indians who had camped there with their families fled in every direction before the troopers' gunfire, the sound of the shots echoing off the stone walls of the canyon. Confusion reigned as women screamed and frightened children struggled desperately to climb the bluffs. Smoke from rifle fire was everywhere as the cavalrymen pursued. Some Indians raced to take shelter behind boulders, others ran shouting toward their herd of horses trying to drive both horses and mules up the canyon. Indian braves, finally abandoning their horses, managed to escape through a pass. They fired down at the troopers while others sought the safety of rock outcroppings along the steep canyon walls.

"After repelling the counterattack, Mackenzie ordered his men to gather all the Indians had left behind them—clothing, food, weapons, cooking utensils, even the tepees. Everything that was essential to their existence the troopers piled in enormous heaps and torched while the Indians who had crept back down the canyon walls watched. Seeing that they had lost all, the Indians banded together for one last courageous attack, only to be driven off again by troopers. Finally the resistance was over. None of the cavalrymen were killed but an untold number of Indians died.

"Mackenzie's men rounded up over 1,400 frightened Indian ponies and formed a living corral around them to begin the twenty-mile march back to the Tule canyon camp. That night the captured horses which had been driven up narrow trails to the bluffs above were placed in the center of camp at the head of the canyon. They were put under heavy guard and surrounded by wagons. He gave first choice of the horses to the scouts, replaced his worn-out cavalry horses, and sold others, giving the proceeds to the troops as extra spending money.

"But Mackenzie did not believe in holding Indian ponies. After breakfast on the morning of September 29th, infantrymen roped the animals left and brought them back to the prairie near the rim of Tule Canyon.

"What a sight those horses must have been—more colors and patterns than you can possibly imagine. Reddish brown with black manes and tails, solid blacks, roans, grays, buckskins, sorrels, pintos with patches of white, black spotted Appaloosas and probably a few palominos. I'm sure there were also some with zebra-type stripes on their legs and shoulders or a black stripe down their backs from mane to tail like their Spanish ancestors."

"I've seen some striped, grandfather," said Patricia.

"Yes, you still see it in some mustangs today," he said looking at her fondly. "Love horses, don't you, honey?" She nodded. Patricia wore a warm bright colored poncho, and the Roundtrees had zipped up their jackets against the chill of the September evening air.

"Well, I don't even like to think about what happened next," said Rodgers.

"Mackenzie gave orders for firing squads to shoot down the herd of horses. Terror stricken, they whinnied wildly, and it was all the troopers could do to control them. Rearing on their hind legs, snorting with fear at the sharp, staccato sound of the gunfire, there was the sound of acre upon acre of dying horses crying out with pain. Over a thousand animals were killed."

"Oh, no!" said Roundtree.

"The gunshots went on from mid-morning until three o'clock that afternoon. Finally all was quiet except for an occasional moan or whinny here and there from ponies that were still alive. For the rest of the day the troopers piled up bodies and left them.

"No one ever moved them and years later the whitened bones of Indian ponies left out here to rot could still be seen. Early farmers hauled them by wagon to Colorado City."

Oklahoma shook his head sadly. "They were paid only about $20 a ton for what had been the Indians' most prized possession."

He tilted his chair back against the front of his ranch house and looked off into the distance thoughtfully.

"The poor horses!" Alan looked sick. "How far was that from here?"

"About a hundred yards." Rodgers suddenly came back to the present. "I'm sorry. It's not a pretty story."

"What about the ghost story part?" asked Roundtree.

"Just a legend. Later people sometimes reported that they had seen a herd of phantom horses on moonlight nights galloping along the rim of Tule Canyon."

"That's interesting," said Mr. Roundtree thoughtfully.

"But why did they shoot all of them?" cried out Alan.

"I hate those men that did that," said Priscilla hotly. "Animals can't defend themselves."

"Well, I'm not sure I can excuse Mackenzie's order even yet. I've thought myself there had to be other options," her grandfather replied. "Why not give some of them to settlers? Any healthy horse was in great demand, so great that they shot a horse thief. But the troopers, in a sense, were at war with the renegade Indians from the reservations, and men don't take a lot of time to think in situations like that. Mackenzie didn't want to risk holding the horses, because he thought the Indians would return, get them and then have the mobility to attack."

"But the Indians were pretty demoralized anyway, weren't they?" asked Roundtree. "Scattered. Without food or supplies?"

"That's true," said Oklahoma.

"And the bones were near this ranch?"

"Yes. For years the skeletons could still be seen strewn across the prairie ... wherever they had fallen," Rodgers said sadly. He gestured off into the darkness.

"Time we all got to bed," said Rodgers. "I've kept you folks up long enough."

Patricia was restless most of the night. Just before daylight she finally slept but her sleep was not a peaceful one. She dreamed that she saw a herd of horses and even heard the sound of their hoofs, but she did not wake until she felt her bed trembling. She got up, parted the curtains and looked out into the bright moonlight. Then she raised the bedroom window, and when she did she heard a thundering sound approaching from the rim of Tule Canyon with a terrible rhythmic, vibrating rumble. Soon she saw the dark shape of a herd of horses, and they were headed straight toward the ranch house. Shivering, she stood in the cold night breeze before the open window watching them thunder toward her.

Galloping swiftly in the moonlight, the herd drew closer, whinnying and bellowing angrily as one horse edged over into another. Hypnotized by the sight, she watched the riderless herd of ghostly chargers with flaming eyes and flashing hooves. A pair of beautiful golden palominos were in the lead, and it seemed to Patricia that they would all soon sweep over her; but still she could not move.

At the last minute the two golden palominos, wheeling in unison, veered away from the house and over the hills—the hills where a century ago they had been shot to death by United States soldiers. Then they were gone.

Dazed, the girl went back to her bed and slept heavily until morning.

After breakfast her grandfather put on a jacket and sat in his rocker on the porch. She went out and sat beside him—an invitation for him to talk but today he said nothing. Finally she broke the silence.

"Have the Roundtrees gone?"

"Yes. Left early. Seems the boy was awake during the night and couldn't get back to sleep. Your grandmother thought I had upset him with my story of the horses."

"Grandfather, something strange happened to me last night."

"What was it?"

"I saw the most beautiful herd of horses."

"Dreamed about them? That's no surprise after our conversation before you went to bed."

"No. This was different. It was a real herd, and the noise shook the house. I think that was what must have upset Alan."

"Was the herd galloping near the rim of Tule Canyon?"

"At first."

"What a coincidence—something similar happened to me."

"Could you pick out any horses from the rest or see the color?" Her knuckles were white as she tightened her fingers on the arms of her chair in suspense.

"In a dream?"

"It wasn't a dream!"

"It's crazy to say this, but I could. There were two horses that stood out from all the rest because they were ahead of the herd."

"What *color* were they?" Patricia asked.

"Golden—a pair of beautiful golden palominos with creamy white tails."

She gave a little gasp. "That's just what I saw!"

"Then perhaps it really wasn't a dream."

He was silent for awhile before he spoke. "I don't know what it was, honey, but I feel a little better about those horses this morning. I think they're galloping in the moonlight somewhere just like they did here in this life."

Her grandfather avoided looking at her, but if he had she would have seen tears in the old pioneer's eyes.

The Ghost of Vallecito

HANK KNOWLES HAD DRIVEN the Butterfield stagecoach for more than a year now. It had been a good year, and he liked driving a route that passed by his home. He and his wife, Jen, and their two children lived in Carrizo, California, and when he stopped there Jen always had a warm meal waiting for him in the adobe fireplace. He enjoyed this brief respite.

His stage route was monotonous, but he couldn't complain about that. As for excitement, the last thing he wanted to hear in the open desert were the dread words, "Throw down the box!" No driver wanted to meet a robber like "Black Bart."

Today the stage lumbered down the rutted wash near Vallecito, California, rolling on its springs. Passengers were lurching from side to side, bumping each other crazily—almost indecorously in the opinion of the ladies sitting next to gentlemen. Up on the high seat sat the driver alone, reins in hand, occasionally cracking his whip. Mostly as a matter of form it would seem, for the horses were already straining and laying into their collars although the road was slightly downgraded.

The new boots Jen had made him buy hurt like fury. The first thing he planned to do at home was to pull them off and drag out the old ones—dusty, with deep furrows across the instep and run-down leather heels. The new ones would become Sunday go-to-meeting boots.

Eastbound to Carrizo, and making good time, he found himself dozing a little for he always became sleepy that time of afternoon. When the stage passed Tres Palmas Spring before dusk, he figured, that with continued luck he should be ahead of schedule. "We will have a stop at Carrizo. You folks can rest your weary bones," said Knowles. There were exclamations of relief. "Remind me to tell you the story of the phantom stage of Carrizo," said Knowles.

"Now, driver. Tell us now!" begged one of the ladies.

"After we leave there will be time enough," he said. "I will show

you where I saw it myself."

Just out of Tres Palmas a rugged, darkly handsome man on a great white stallion shouted a greeting and galloped up, staying beside his stage. The next thing Knowles noticed about him was that he was a superb rider and gentle with his horse. It was also obvious he knew the area well. Now driving a stage can be a lonely thing and the stranger was a good talker.

"Have you heard the story of the wandering skeleton seen on the desert at night? Eight feet tall and the man who saw it was near scared out of his boots." At the very least the stories of his companion would keep him awake. They talked about some Butterfield drivers the rider seemed to know here and there, so the time passed pleasantly enough.

Then, suddenly, in the middle of the hot desert afternoon, three horsemen dashed out from behind a rock outcropping, and the next thing he knew four guns were aimed at his heart. Though he was terrified, Knowles felt a curious sense of excitement. Every driver anticipates the day something like this will happen. He never knows how he will react.

"Put up your hands!" shouted the leader of the trio galloping forward. They were joined by the horseman who had ridden beside the driver. Knowles reined in his horses, and the stage jerked to a halt. He had a gun but the gun would be too dangerous to try to reach. It had slipped back under the seat. Everything was happening much too quickly. The other course was to whip his horses and make a dash for it. If he did that they would probably shoot him and some passengers might be killed as well. Even if they didn't get him with their first shots, it certainly wouldn't take men long on horseback to catch up with a stage.

He seemed to tingle all over.

"Now. Throw down the box," ordered an authoritative voice. It had a certain lethal quality and belonged to a darkly tanned man with gray hair. Beside him rode a youngish man on a bay and on the other side, a Mexican. Hesitating only briefly, Knowles pulled out the box, laden with gold, from under the seat. He dropped it on the ground, and then his hands went down to his sides.

"Keep those hands up!" barked the man on the white horse. He did.

The bandits, who all wore handkerchiefs over their noses and mouths, relieved the passengers of their money, jewelry, and any personal effects that caught their fancy. Turning his head very slightly, Knowles looked for the horseman who had ridden with him. The fellow had been part of a trap set for the stage and its passengers, thought Knowles, for he had thoroughly distracted his attention from the road ahead. Although the brigands must have been lying in wait for him for some time, he might have seen something had he been watching more intently.

"All right. Let's go, men," shouted the bandit chief. Wheeling his horse around, his men following, he galloped off toward Vallecito, and with them galloped the horseman that had ridden side by side with the stage. The bandits had taken $65,000 in gold.

Sighting carefully, Knowles aimed at the man riding the bay and fired as they rode off. He thought he got him. Unharnessing one of the horses, he rode after the bandits and stopped to examine the body. He found not one but two dead men. His own bullet had found its mark and the rider of the bay, a boy of barely twenty, lay dead. A few feet away the Mexican was sprawled on his back, a red stain on his chest, his eyes staring sightlessly at the sky. Knowles, seeing a heavy gold ring on the man's hand, reached down. He pulled it off and slipped it into his pocket.

It appeared as though the bandit chief—a greedy, merciless sort—had deliberately killed one of his own men so the booty could be divided one less way. When Knowles returned to the coach, he did not mention that a second man had been shot in order to spare the nervous passengers.

The stop at Carrizo was desperately needed now. Two of Knowles's passengers needed to be seen by a doctor; one was a hysterical young woman and the other an elderly man who kept his hand to his chest. A rider was sent on to Vallecito, toward which the bandits had fled, to report the robbery.

Somewhere in the vicinity of the town, the two bandits must have cached their loot. They went on to the stagecoach station and ordered whiskey after whiskey, but as they drank they began to quarrel.

"You never want to be part of the action, Dan," said Sean O'Hara accusingly to his brother.

"What do you mean?" Dan replied angrily. "I was the one that rode beside the driver and set him up for you."

"Have you ever taken on the driver of a stage single-handed? Frisked the passengers? No. You're too big a coward!"

"Well, at least I don't shoot men in the back!"

"You mangy dog," Sean said contemptuously. "I'm going out to take care of my horse now, and when I come back we'll settle this for good."

An hour later when Sean O'Hara came back he was riding his big bay bareback. He rode it up to the Vallecito station, shot Dan's white stallion tethered outside, kicked in the front door, and fired two shots at his brother, hitting him in the chest. Daniel reeled and fell, but as he did so he aimed and fired his own gun. The bullet struck Sean behind the right ear, and he dropped with a cry to the hard-packed dirt floor.

As both O'Hara brothers lay mortally wounded in the station, a crowd began gathering around them. They died within minutes of each other, leaving the site of their treasure unknown.

It was later told in the valley that near the Vallecito station around midnight the ghost of a great white horse was sometimes seen galloping by. Those who heard about it said that the horse must be guarding the spot where the treasure was buried.

Hearing about the sightings, Frank Knowles decided that he would spend a night at Vallecito station in hopes of seeing the ghost and recovering the bandits' gold. They had probably cached some from other robberies as well, but if there were any passengers still to be found who were riding his stage on the day of the holdup, he would see to it that whatever gold they had lost was returned. Still blaming himself, he could not forget he had allowed himself to be taken in by the man on the white stallion riding at his side.

Positioning himself outside the station, Knowles sat with his back against the adobe wall of the building to wait. He had his own horse tethered close beside him so that he could leap upon it and follow the phantom steed.

He had ridden for a considerable distance that day and was so tired that he could scarcely stay awake. Suddenly, out of nowhere, he saw the ghost of a great white horse appear, and he jumped upon his mount. On the white horse came, galloping swiftly toward him across the sand. He reined his horse in, for he was in the center of the road before the station, and it would surely run him down! The horse had almost reached him when a mist began to gather around it and the muscular form of the stallion blurred, appearing to be part of a luminous, shifting cloud. Knowles's large bay was tossing its head this way and that and neighing nervously as Knowles turned him in the direction of the phantom steed, but the horse galloped after it.

Knowles pursued the spectre of the white horse, pushing his bay to a hard gallop. They had raced after it for perhaps a mile and a half from the Vallecito station when the cloud surrounding the spectral stallion stopped near a large cottonwood tree. Knowles believed that neither his nor any other horse alive could have caught up with it had it not been meant to happen. It was the great white stallion of the bandit who had driven along the stage beside him. Had it led him to the gold?

After that night, some people in Carrizo winked knowingly and said Knowles had succeeded in finding the buried treasure. No one knew for sure, but it did not go unnoticed that from that time forth Hank Knowles had more money to spend than any other Butterfield driver. When he wore his expensive new boots or his wife was arrayed in silk and lace there were those who talked. "Hank knows a ghost horse when he sees one," they said, winking behind his back, "and he found the treasure." But none came forward to question him.

FARM ANIMAL GHOSTS

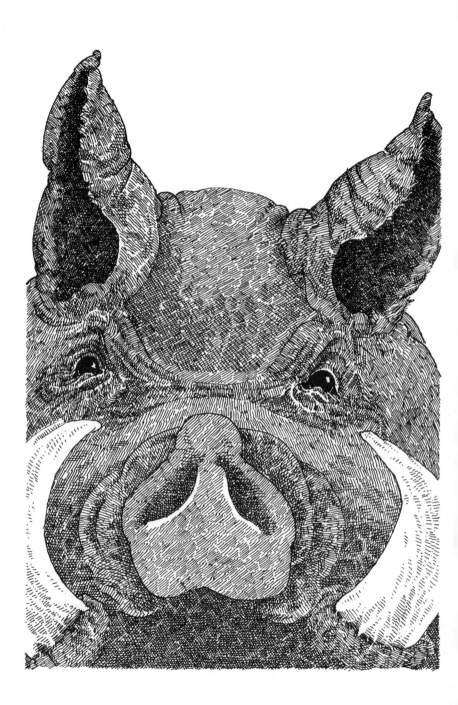

The Black Pig

THE BOY'S STRAIGHT HAIR was coarse and black. His nose protruded like a snout above the red-lipped mouth, buck teeth, and almost nonexistent chin. Sometimes the very sight of him made Otto angry and he would rail at his brother over nothing. Their father had died in the Kaiser's war and their mother had passed away a year later, leaving only Otto to take care of Johann … forever and ever and ever he often thought.

Johann was three years older, eager to help and generally cheerful. He would go out scavenging for wood and pieces of coal to augment their meager supply of fuel, sweep the floor which he kept compulsively clean, and wash the cook pot and plates after each meal. He did the cooking and never seemed to notice that when Otto helped himself to stew he would invariably take any choice bits of meat for himself, leaving the less desirable pieces for him.

There was no indoor plumbing so Johann washed their bedding down on the rocks of the stream. No matter that the weather was sometimes so cold his knuckles were cracked and raw from rubbing the sheets on the stones, the boy considered it his responsibility, and just the doing of these simple tasks made him happy.

The brothers were very different in coloring and body build, Johann stocky and somewhat awkward, Otto tall, blond, and heavily muscled from physical labor—all he had found to do since the war. But he never forgot his father's words to him. "Otto, you are the one with the mind. You will be a man of worth someday."

And now and then he would add, "Had it not been for Doctor Katz attending your mother, Johann would have perished right then. Do you know, sometimes Johann turns to me and says, 'Fader, I enjoy my life.'" Herr Kruger's voice trailed off and his eyes would grow moist. As for Otto, he wished his brother had never lived.

He thought about how impoverished everyone had been since World War I. Even the wealthy were still living in greatly reduced circumstances, and in the early months, many of the poor had died from malnutrition and lack of medical attention. He himself was employed with a work crew, but soon they would be leaving for a part of Germany near the French border. What a fine opportunity to leave the country; if he could just get to France he could stow away on a ship to America.

You are the one with the mind, Otto. His father's words echoed over and over in his mind, and he knew that he, Otto, was worthy of a better life than this—a decent job, a good wife, a comfortable home.

He thought of these things for the thousandth time tonight as they sat eating at the kitchen table. "Jo-ho," as he called himself, because it was difficult for the boy to enunciate his words clearly, held out a bowl of boiled potatoes. There was only one left and with a fork he placed this last potato, like an offering, on Otto's plate, the small, stupid eyes gazing at him lovingly as if waiting for a word of thanks or praise. None was forthcoming.

Sometimes, when he looked at his brother it seemed to Otto the young man resembled a pig. There was the pink skin, the receding mouth with the prominent canine tooth on either side. They reminded him of tusks. He ate in silence.

November, the time for his work crew to leave his area, drew nearer, and Otto realized he should look for another job, but he delayed. In late October the winter's first snow began to fall, coating the tall dark evergreens that grew close around the house. Opening the front door, Otto saw that a fine white powder was already clinging to the rough-hewn gray boards of the shack, and he shivered realizing how much the temperature had dropped.

"Jo-ho, we do not have enough wood left, and the snow grows deeper," he called to his brother.

"Ja. I get some right away," answered Johann obediently, putting on their father's old Army overcoat and tying a scarf about his head. He went out into the dusk. All the wood from near the cabin had been gathered and Johann would have a walk of more than a mile to the forest to search for more. Otto locked the door and decided to start supper. He placed some sliced potatoes in a pan on a trivet over the hot coals in the fireplace, stirred them, and a few minutes later added two pieces of good German sausage. When the tantalizing aroma of the sausage and golden brown hue of the potatoes indicated they were done, he filled his plate. Looking down at what was left, Otto paused thoughtfully, and then, with one firm motion, he scraped the pan clean and ate until there was no more.

Wind moaned and snow filled the cracks and crannies outside the house. Stretched on the floor before the fire, Otto struggled to read a dog-eared book about America that a fellow crew member had forgotten and left at the work site. Staring fixedly at the pictures, he abandoned himself to his obsession—the United States—recognizing a word here and there. I-l-l-i-n-o-i-s he spelled out. In the picture the countryside looked surprisingly like the land around him. If only he could get there, that is where he would head for—Illinois.

An hour passed ... an hour and a half. Johann still had not returned. Suddenly Otto heard a thud at the door and automatically started to rise—then he hesitated. He lowered himself back into his chair and waited. The sound came again. It was followed by a desperate pounding and a voice crying out indistinguishable words. Otto tried to tell himself that it might be some rascal seeking shelter on this cold night, some tramp who might be dangerous, but all the time he knew—oh, he knew.

And then, almost carried away by the wind, came terrified cries, "Jo-ho. I Jo-ho. Let me in, brother." Otto did not stir.

His face was set in a hard, cruel expression. His hands clutched the edge of the chair seat until his knuckles grew white as he sat there immobile while the sounds outside grew weaker and weaker. Finally a scraping noise like something hard being rubbed back and forth across the door started and seemed to go on and on. He had to end this. Rising from the chair, he opened the door. There was Johann. Lying on the step, his fingers grasped a piece of the wood he had gathered and he was scraping it against the door. His brother's face was a mask of snow crystals covering the freezing human flesh. A tuft of stiff black hair, white with snow, stuck out from beneath the scarf on his head.

Otto steeled himself for what he must do. Reaching down beneath the collar of the old Army coat, his strong hands found Johann's neck. He squeezed and squeezed and squeezed. Guttural cries rose above the noise of the wind, and finally he felt the heavy body go limp. He let it fall to the ground, convinced that the falling snow would cover it nicely. A more permanent solution could be worked out at dawn.

Heaping the largest logs he had on the fire, he wrapped himself in two blankets, curled up near the stone hearth, and slept soundly.

He stirred when the sharp edge of cold gray light appeared above the dark trees, his waking thought what to do with his brother's body. Where but under the hearthstone, Otto said to himself smiling grimly. According to the old stories wasn't that always the place a murderer buried his victim? But surely he was not a murderer. He had only done what he had to do. As his father had so often said, he was the one with the good mind, and the fact that Johann even possessed a life had only been due to the act of a sentimental old fool like Dr. Katz. He was free of Johann. Free forever!

Despite the dark task that lay ahead of him, Otto was elated. He began to excavate under the hearthstone. With a crowbar, it was not so difficult to get the stone out but under it Otto found the clay rock-studded and so hard a shovel scarcely dented it. He tried a pick. After two hours' work he had made only a shallow depression. Would it conceal the body? He couldn't be certain until he tried it for fit. He must go out and bring Johann in.

Opening the front door for the first time that morning he saw that the sun was melting the snow and spots of dung colored earth could be seen. His heart seemed to stop. The body was not there!

Otto Kruger had no time for an extensive search. Everything would point to him as his brother's murderer, and he felt a strangling sense of fear. He must flee Germany immediately. Hands trembling, he stuffed a bundle of marks into the secret pocket in his work jacket. It would buy him food until he could get to the nearest port city and hire on a ship—a ship to America.

In Brighton, Illinois, the man who left behind him the name of Otto Kruger and now called himself Charles Rice felt at home. Many other Germans had settled here. Employed as a baker, he lived frugally, saved his money, and within a few years he was the owner of his own bakery. Marrying not long after his arrival, he and Gertrude became the parents of a daughter, Kate, and later two sons. They named the older boy Hans, and perhaps because memories of the old country were not as strong, the father wanted his younger son named Charles. Rice was prosperous by now and had more time for his second child. He doted upon Charles. While the little boy learned to walk and later play on his swings in the back yard of the big, gray frame house the Rices watched happily.

At least they were happy until a strange event occurred.

One day, as Charles played outdoors, they noticed a monstrous black pig following him. Mrs. Rice saw the animal first through their kitchen window, and thought it had strayed from a nearby farm. When she went out and approached it the pig eyed her with a strange, almost pleading look in its small eyes, but as she came close, it would run off into the woods. To her it did not seem unfriendly—merely strange and somewhat frightening. But when Charles Rice, Sr. tried to catch the pig, it ran at him with such malevolence that he retreated hastily. Inquiries among neighbors as to the ownership of the black pig drew only a shake of the head and a bewildered look.

"*Vas is los mitt der pig?*" people would respond curiously.

Those who saw the animal following the child asked his father about this strange phenomena, and he became greatly agitated.

"You have talked about this to the neighbors," he shouted at his wife angrily. She shook her head, for it was apparent to many without her speaking of it. Now Rice ceased to talk about it even to her.

But the child, Charles, could not be hushed. When he started to school he told his friends about this strange thing and how he was followed about. The boys looked at each other, laughed and poked fun at him. No one would believe such a story.

"Why don't you bring the pig to school?" they jeered.

"I can't. So far it hasn't followed me away from the house. You'll see. Come and spend the night with me."

Three of the boys said they would go. After supper they arrived at the Rice house to spend the night with Charles in his small attic bedroom. One of them was a boy, John Vannaham, and years later he told it this way.

"We asked Charles to turn off the lamp but he wouldn't, saying, 'I let it burn all night because when the pig comes, I don't want to be in the dark.' Then he said, 'If the lamp goes out, the pig will appear, and I will begin to strangle. Then you must *call my name three times.*' We just snickered."

"We were all sound asleep when a noise like a loud bounce on the stairs woke us," said John.

"Then the lamp went out. We began to giggle thinking this was going to be great fun. There was a sharp incessant clicking sound in the hall. Our door flew open. Suddenly it wasn't funny. We heard Charles make horrible noises like he was strangling, and we were scared. Aided by the faint circle of moonlight that came into the room through a small window in the gable we saw a monstrous black pig.

"We tried to catch it, but just when we thought we had our hands on it and were actually touching its coarse bristles it would slip away from us and appear just out of reach. It jumped on the foot of Charles's bed, and the dreadful noises in his throat grew worse."

Frightened as the boys were, they remembered his instructions.

"If the lamp goes out, the pig will appear, and I will begin to strangle. Then you must *call my name three times.*"

"Charles! Charles! Charles!" they shouted.

"The black pig suddenly turned, and hurtling through the air from the bed was out the door and clattering down the stairs. After that we did not doubt there really was a black pig," said John Vannaham. The boys never spent another night with Charles Rice.

Whether the lamp was lit or unlit didn't keep the animal from appearing in the terrified boy's room. Charles began to believe the black pig would follow him forever, although it did not always make itself visible.

The Rices became more solitary, and Charles' father, who even before this had never been a jolly, talkative man, gradually grew more hostile. Charles, convinced that he had a spell on him, sought out the pastor of a small Lutheran church in Brighton and asked him about ways to remove spells. The pastor made a thorough investigation of each floor of the Rice home and spoke of sensing something foul and evil within the house. Charles Rice, Sr. flew into a rage, ordered him to leave, and threatened to kill him if he ever came back.

A few years later Charles went alone to visit his older brother in Kansas, hoping that the change would rid him of his pursuer. He entered his bedroom that night, and lighting the lamp found the room warm and the colors of the quilt cheerful. Feeling as if a heavy weight had been lifted from his heart, Charles settled himself in the comfortable feather bed for a good night's sleep. All went well. To his relief the second night was like the first. But this deliverance was not to last. On the third night the lamp suddenly went out, and the young man heard the sharp clatter of hooves on the stairs. The monstrous pig rushed into his room and the terrified Charles was sure he would choke to death. From the room below his brother heard all the commotion and the horrible sounds of strangling. Rushing upstairs he shouted, "Charles! Charles! Charles!" He hurled himself across the room at the creature, but it was gone.

The black pig vanished from his brother's home forever, but the haunting of Charles was not to cease easily.

On the way home to Brighton he stopped in Alton, Illinois, to visit his sister, Kate. After first talking with his brother-in-law down at the barn, he went up to the house. He spent the night quite peacefully, and the next day went on to his father's home in Brighton. On the third night after he had left them, his sister's family was awakened by the most terrible noises coming from the barn—cattle mooing, calves bleating, bulls bellowing, horses whinnying. The animals began striking their hooves frantically against the walls of their stalls, trying to kick them down.

Father and sons threw on their clothes and raced to the barn. When they reached it, all was quiet, but by now they heard sounds of a terrible commotion coming from the direction of the house. Racing back, the husband found the chairs knocked about the living room and his wife lying in a faint upon the floor. He looked up from her body to see the black pig in the front hall bounding up the stairs toward the room where Charles had slept.

The black pig had traveled three days to reach the house in Kansas and three days back, and from then on Charles noticed it always took the pig three days to reach him no matter where he went.

No one could catch it or shoot it. Meanwhile the pig appeared to be growing larger. This continued for many years, Charles finally becoming so strange in his behavior that his father was forced to take him to a sanatorium. When he was admitted, Mr. Rice, a hollow-eyed, emaciated man who jumped nervously at every sound, explained his son's malady to the director and his assistant.

"He thinks he is being pursued by a black pig," said the father in a halting voice, his eyes darting this way and that, as if he himself might see the pig at any moment. "A type of insanity," he explained. "I hope that your physicians here can cure it."

With difficulty the director hid a smile. He nodded reassuringly and after the elder Rice left said to his assistant, "Mark my words, that old fellow will be with us soon, too."

"Yes. I'm afraid so. The father appears far madder than the son," observed the other.

At the institution nothing changed for poor Charles. The drama, according to him, would repeat itself again and again—first the sound of hooves striking the floor, then the lamp flickering until the flame went out, leaving the room in a thick, suffocating darkness, and finally terrified, choking sounds coming from his throat.

Rice would implore each new night attendant to call his name three times if he heard sounds coming from his room. This plea was for the most part ignored, but occasionally, someone would humor him, calling out his name three times and the next day tell friends on the staff, "I scared off that pig last night." This jest always elicited a smile.

Charles Rice spent two months in the institution. On his last night there, after he prepared for bed, he must have thought he heard the approaching clatter of hooves and then the flicker of the kerosene lamp. Perhaps he believed that the flame would catch up as it usually did. If so, he had a brief moment of hope before the lamp went out, leaving the room in total darkness.

Next morning the attendant knocked on young Rice's door. He recalled that he had been dozing in his chair when sometime after midnight he heard the familiar anguished cries coming from the room. He was sleepy and did not play what he had come to consider the game of calling out Rice's name three times.

Now, receiving no answer, he shouted in fun, "Charles, Charles, Charles!"

His patient did not reply, and the impatient attendant opened the door to look in. He saw an empty bed. The bedclothes were in terrible disarray, the sheets torn like the sails of a ship that has gone through a hurricane. Half-concealed by a large oak bureau, Rice's still figure was on the floor. Staring down at him the horrified attendant saw the man's bruised throat, purplish-black protruding tongue and the face contorted in mortal terror. Charles Rice had made a desperate fight for life. Arms, already stiff from rigor mortis, were thrust out from his body as if to ward off something unspeakable.

The coroner who arrived to examine Rice and ascertain the cause of death was much astonished at the sight before him. Tracked all over the white bedspread, even upon the pale, upraised palms of the dead man's hands, with which he had apparently tried to shield himself, were the well-defined hoofprints of a pig.

Stubborn as a Mule

ILSE TURNED DOWN THE WICK of the kerosene lamp on the kitchen table as soon as the light of the December dawn invaded the room. She was a practical, unimaginative woman, and Jacob Tinker appreciated that, but today he was angry with her.

"At least Hans and Neil and Ernest believe me, Ilse. They all saw it!"

"Now don't start talking foolishness again this morning, Jacob," she said.

For the hundredth time Jacob wished he hadn't told his wife about the events of last Saturday.

"I am already tired this morning, and I am barely on my way," he thought as he walked toward the town of Albion. He shouldn't have said a word to his wife in the first place, and he wouldn't have if he hadn't mentioned to her a year or two before that John Brissenden, a respected man in the community, had shocked everyone one morning at the store.

It all began when Neil Neilson, Klaus Earnhardt, Ernest Bromfeld, himself and John all sitting around the stove reminiscing about how they happened to come to southern Illinois. Brissenden, who seldom volunteered much of a personal nature, became more expansive.

"You know, it seems a long time ago now when Elizabeth and I left England. It was back in 1819. During those weeks on the ship our romance began, and we got married right after we arrived in this country. I guess because the others were heading for southern Illinois, we decided to come too."

"This is a fine place," said Neil, who had arrived only five years before from Sweden, and the men in the circle nodded in agreement. Then Klaus spoke up saying that his brother from Germany had just settled near Chicago, and he was planning to visit him for the first time. He added, as he often did, "The good Lord willing."

Brissenden just couldn't let that pass.

"When you receive the Lord's permission to go, let me know," he said with that mocking smile of his.

The group of men looked at him, shocked at his irreverence. Albion was a God-fearing, church-going community, and Elizabeth Brissenden, along with the Brissenden children, were at services every Sunday—but not John.

"I just meant that all of our plans are tentative," said Klaus. "None of us know how long we will be here or when we will leave this world for the next."

"The next world? And where is this next world you are so sure of, my friend?" asked Brissenden.

"That's not for us to question," injected Klaus Earnhardt, a shade piously. "It's enough to know that God has prepared a place—"

Brissenden cut him right off. "And who has ever seen this place to be sure it's there?"

No one answered, and he looked around him triumphantly.

"If this God of yours is really thinking about our needs, why does a good man like Hans Schnabel get caught in a snowstorm and die, leaving here to go home from his son-in-law's funeral? He was to return and help his daughter move back to Virginia with her children."

"It was his time to go," replied Neilson, a devout Lutheran.

"I see," said John Brissenden, "but the wrong time for Helga and her two little ones. Isn't that right?"

Neilson's face turned red. "I am only telling you what the Holy Book says."

"Well, I say if there is a God, why doesn't he make sense!"

"Maybe he isn't accountable to you," Jacob said quietly.

Brissenden went on blustering. "Friend, you mean that we will know all these things in the next world. Baah! What if I tell you there is no next world!"

His audience fairly cringed, and Klaus looked up at the white painted planks above his head as if this blasphemy would cause the ceiling to be rent apart by lightning at any moment.

"You've been talking this way for years, John," Jacob said from behind the oak counter. "If your wife, Elizabeth, comes into the store weeping and tells us you died the night before, I think we will all wonder about you, my friend."

Brissenden looked at him with a quizzical expression. "I see what you mean. I have been stubborn, haven't I? Stubborn as a mule." And then a thought seemed to strike him. He paused.

"I guess there is only one way to settle this, and that is to prove beyond a doubt whether there is or is not a hereafter."

His friends, who had long tried to convince him, looked puzzled.

"Whatever is the case, I shall prove it once and for all."

"And just how will you do that?" asked Jacob calmly as he shelved some bales of cambric a customer had left upon the counter.

Brissenden rested his chin in his hands musing in silence. No one spoke. Then he raised his head and looked around him at each of his friends. When he was sure they were hanging on every word he began.

"I intend to prove this one way or another as soon as I die, and I shall tell you how. I know I've been stubborn about it, so, if there really is any life after death, when I come back I shall come back as a mule."

There was a startled gasp, and then someone guffawed.

"No. I mean it. Let me see." He was silent for a moment, thinking.

"Let's make it a white one. Now, to be sure you know it's me and not just an ordinary stray mule, I shall do certain things."

He stopped to relight his pipe, and the men shifted their positions uneasily.

"My spirit will go to the corner of the square," he said, gesturing toward the northeast, "right in front of where my house is located, and it will bray a few times like a mule. Then, ask me if that is my house and I shall bray three times in reply." John Brissenden grinned, a grin so wide that his broken tooth showed, as if at the idea of himself braying was highly amusing. Then he continued.

"If a mule does not show up, you'll know I've been right: there is no such thing as life after death. But if a mule does appear at the corner in front of my house braying, you have been right, and I have been wrong. The white mule will be my spirit returned from that world of the hereafter you have tried to convince me about for so many years."

"If I am wrong," he added more seriously, "*please* do not forget to feed me."

With that, Brissenden gathered up his purchases and strode out of the store. The others, subdued, left soon. That night when Jacob went home, he related the conversation to his wife.

"You men should have better things to do than sit around that store listening to John Brissenden blaspheme," she said indignantly.

Several years passed and Elizabeth Brissenden predeceased her husband. His wife's death did not change the skeptical Brissenden one whit. He continued going to the store, meeting his friends each morning, living complacently on in the house on the square with several of his children who were still unmarried. He was a well thought-of man, if something of an enigma to others.

On the morning of the 2nd of December 1872, for the first time anyone could remember, John Brissenden did not join the other men at the store to talk about the crops and exchange local gossip. He had passed away in the night at the age of seventy-six years, one month, and twenty-five days.

His friends of a lifetime held their hands out toward the warmth of the stove and spoke quietly. They all knew old John's lack of faith, but no one mentioned it. It just didn't seem right to talk like that about the dead. Neilson wondered aloud why Brissenden had never used any of his money to go back to visit Kent County or Nottinghamshire, England where he and his wife were from. Others recalled how he got his start working hard for other people until he made enough money to leave the house on Meridian Road in the country and build the home on courthouse square in Albion.

Saturday morning, following Brissenden's funeral, Jacob Tinker arrived at his store early, as was his custom, to check his merchandise for the day. He arranged pears, potatoes, turnips, and other winter vegetables in front of the frosted window panes of his store and placed two bags of coal on each side of the double front doors. No one was yet in sight on the main street of the small midwest town of Albion but it would not be long until some of the merchant's first customers arrived. He was ready for them.

Jacob picked up a pear, which had been wrapped in paper to keep it fresh and succulent, polished it on the sleeve of his plaid flannel shirt, and bit into it. The crunch of the hard, crisp fruit broke the silence. Just when he was thinking how he enjoyed this brief solitude before the business of the day began, the stillness was broken.

Clop, clop, clip, clop, clip, clop. He could hear the sound of slow, rhythmic hoofbeats approaching but at first did not see the source. Then in the distance he saw a lone white mule without a rider. It was doubtless a stray that had wondered off from some farm, and the farmer would probably be coming after it. Snatching his jacket from his chair behind the counter along with a bridle, he hurried out to catch the animal so it would not block the wagons that crowded Main Street on market day.

He would tie it to the rail in front of the store, and its owner would probably see it there. As he hurried in pursuit he was joined by several other men who had the same idea, and soon there was a small band following the animal. The mule had increased its pace and was heading in the direction of the public square. When he reached it he headed for the northeast corner of the square and then turned around and appeared to look at them in surprise as if noticing his entourage for the first time. His lips spread wide to show large yellow teeth, and the men shrank back.

But the baring of his teeth did not seem to be an unfriendly gesture, for it was followed by a loud and prolonged bray. Then the mule erupted into a succession of hee-haws climaxed by the noisiest and most jarring bray the men had ever heard.

Jacob Tinker abandoned his belief that this mule was a stray.

"It's him," he said suddenly.

"It's who?" asked a man who had just recently moved to Albion.

"That is John Brissenden."

The stranger's mouth fell open. "Mr. Tinker, you mean this animal is named John Brissenden."

"No. I don't meant that its name is John Brissenden. I meant that it is John Brissenden," he replied impatiently. "I mean it's his spirit."

The newcomer edged away from Jacob, looking at him strangely, and the storekeeper said, stumbling over his explanation, "I don't know how to say what I mean—only that he told us if he came back it would be as a mule."

Leaving the fellow to think what he would, Jacob Tinker pushed his way forward and took the bridle to lead the animal out of the square, but the white mule stubbornly stood firm. People began to gather around them. An agitated Klaus Earnhardt who had made his way through the crowd seized Jacob by the arm.

"That's him! Do you remember that morning in the store? He is right where he said he would be, at the northeast corner of the square."

The men stood around watching, and the mule began to crop grass.

"I've got to get back to my store. Will you keep an eye on him, Klaus?"

"Here comes Neil. We can take turns. But I don't think he's going anywhere."

At the store Jacob hurriedly ate his sauerkraut and sausage sandwich, and pouring some oats into a feed bag, he started back to the square. The mule was still standing there, and he had just given it the oats when a small boy struck the mule's flank with a switch. In return one of the rear hoofs lashed out at him. The boy jumped hurriedly out of range. Jacob noted that it was not a vicious kick but more like a warning.

Earnhardt returned, this time bringing Neil along.

"I'm going to ask him the question," said Jacob.

"What question?" said Neil.

"Don't you remember?" Jacob stepped up beside the mule and pointing toward the Brissenden home asked, "Is that your house?"

The mule brayed three times, and the face of the men registered shock.

"Try it again," said Klaus. "Let's be sure."

"Is that your house?" repeated Jacob and this time he emphasized the question by pointing toward the large two-story house across the street. Again the mule brayed three times, and this time Jacob noticed that one of the animal's back teeth was broken off. *Just like John Brissenden's,* he thought with a start of recognition.

After this Jacob's wife finally believed he was right, although many people derided the possibility that the mule contained the spirit of their late respected citizen. Jacob continued to muse about the situation. If the mule wasn't a supernatural creature why didn't anyone miss it? How did it arrive out of nowhere at the square in Albion, and why, although untethered and free to roam, did it remain right in front of Brissenden's house, as if to convince all doubters who it was and why it was there.

The men saw to it that the strange mule was faithfully fed and watered, Jacob among them. In his mind he could still hear John Brissenden's plea, "If I am wrong, *please* do not forget to feed me."

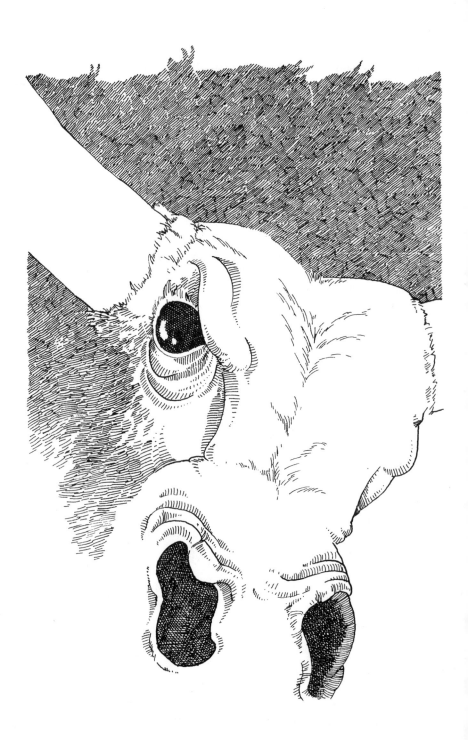

Stampede Mesa

TEXAN ABE SLAUGHTER HAD VISITED many a cattle town, and in recent years he kept swearing, "This is going to be the last one!" But despite his age and some apprehensions, here he was going to another one.

Abilene, Ellsworth, Wichita, Caldwell, and Dodge were the great cattle towns of the West, and he had seen them all. They gave off a raw, crude energy he could feel in his bones. He always knew they were getting close to the end of the trail when he smelled the pungent stench of the stockyards. The cowhand's spirits rose with relief. He could see those cattle towns now—surrounded by pleasant farms, they were teeming, rowdy places full of saloons, dance halls and brothels spilling out music, laughter, and raucous cowhands into muddy streets.

It was a new year, a new herd, a new boss, and the white-haired old cowpunch was on the trail again. He was heading for Dodge, the Queen of Cow Towns. The long, dusty Texas trail led toward Caprock and the high plains. In the late afternoon the cattle—about 1,500 steers—and the men who drove them approached a mesa. At its base was a river where cattle and men could quench their thirst, and on top of it the grazing was unsurpassed.

"We'll hold 'em up there on that mesa, boys," said the new trail boss.

To the cowboy's surprise, Abe, whose job it was to take care of the horses, protested, "There's still plenty of places to hold these cattle down the trail, Grady. Let's not hold 'em up thar."

"What in tarnation, Abe!" burst out Grady Sherman. Several cowboys muttered angrily. Both men and cattle were tired. "We got a fine river, good grass, and it don't suit you?"

"You done forgot that stampede in '91, Grady? It's been ten years, but I still got my bad knee to remind me, and I'm lucky to be alive."

"You're a cranky old ramudero!" said Grady, calling him the name for horse wranglers they had all had picked up from the Mexicans, and turning abruptly he strode toward the river.

Thirsty cattle were already crowding into the water. It was Grady's job to see to two things: that the more timid took their turn drinking—some had to be coaxed—and that the herd didn't start on its way until the last animal's thirst was quenched. Then there were always some cows who wanted space around them when they drank that couldn't be hurried. He knew his job. The only complaint voiced so far by Sherman's cowboys was, "He can be a stubborn cuss."

Uncle Abe watched the sunburned Grady drink greedily, shed his clothes on the ground and with a loud whoop of delight splash into the river. He came up grinning and shaking the water from his curly black hair like a dog from its coat. As the cattle waded in gratefully drinking the cool water of the Blanco, Abe shook his head resignedly and checked his saddle horses.

Grady knew that there were other sites along this trail to hold the cattle for the night, but that day they had endured twelve hot, dusty miles crawling along at about two miles an hour, having to take time out for watering and for the calves to keep up. He was more than ready to make camp when he saw the hillside sloping gently up to a mesa—cattle preferred a slope—and on top of it good grazing. This, he figured, was the best site a trail boss could ask for, and Abe was a superstitious old man. The cattle would graze their way up the slope to the top of the mesa where they would be bedding down becoming more familiar with it every step of the way. That would make them less likely to scare at night.

Accustomed to managing large herds, Grady thought like a trail master. He had his larger plan in mind from the start. Keep the animals calm and contented until they arrived at their destination hundreds of miles away. The animals should be in better condition than when they started traveling. "When they run they run off tallow," he would say to his cowboys. See to it they got plenty of water, grass, sleep and no wasted motion so they would maintain their weight and make money for the owner. If his steers were heading north he wanted them to graze as they moved north—walking slowly in the direction they were headed.

It was Abe's first time to be part of one of Sherman's outfits, and his skill as a trail boss remained to be proved. Abe tried to put aside his misgivings about the mesa. Like everyone else, he was coated with grime and tuckered out. There were ten men in the outfit—Grady, the cook; seven cowboys, two of whom were point men riding on each side at the front to direct the herd; and himself.

I've been a wrangler for so many years that sometimes I feel like I'm kin to these horses, thought Abe as he began unsaddling them. Abe was responsible on this trip for the sixty horses which the cowboys rode in rotation. He knew every horse in his remuda by name, and he knew how to control it. Turning them loose so that they could graze freely, Abe carefully checked the condition of each animal. He blazed out angrily at a cowboy who had been hard on the horse he rode. That kind of fellow wouldn't have a job long. He'd see to it.

Going over to Minnie, he gave her some sugar and stroked her neck. He had a particular fondness for his white bell mare. The horses regarded her the way a flock does a sheep dog. *Tinkle, tinkle,* would go the bell hanging from Minnie's neck as she walked along the trail, and the majority of the horses would follow, tails flicking back and forth right in time to the regular clink of the bell. That night they made camp near the Blanco River about eighteen miles from the cap rock of Blanco Canyon. Hunkering down beside the campfire, the men began to swap stories over beans, bacon, bread, and coffee.

The talk turned to stampedes. Cattle stampedes were always a fascinating subject among cowboys, and there were many reasons for such a disaster. Sometimes the real one was hard to figure. It was an experience that novice cowboys hoped for and experienced ones dreaded.

The cook joined in. "I've known a new cowboy to dismount too close to the cattle and just his horse, shaking the empty saddle and rattlin' stirrups, could start 'em runnin'."

"That's right," nodded Grady, "and don't forget to light any matches with your back turned. Protect that flame with your hands, boys, so the cows don't see it."

"Ever heared of a skunk flicking his tail across the nose of a sleeping steer," said another cowboy, "and frightening the steer so bad he jumps to his feet? Before you know it the whole herd is off an' running."

"Yup," agreed one of the older and wiser point men. "Or it might be that one of 'em smelt an Indian when they're used to the odor of white men. Anything that's unfamiliar. It's scary 'cause you never know what can do it. It can happen so fast."

Then the cowboy they called Smoky who had been staring at the old wrangler said, "Whatsa matter, Abe? Why you sportin' such a glum face?"

"Guess I just don't like this campsite," replied Abe. "That mesa up there ain't no place to hold cattle." Tilting his head back, he drained the last drop of coffee from his tin cup as if to emphasize the words.

"Not a better place to hold a herd, boys," said Grady Sherman in rebuttal. "Bed 'em down on that slope where they're grazin' right now, and in the mornin' we can water 'em again in the river before we leave on the drive."

"Yeah. Those steep bluffs to the south are a natural barrier to their wanderin' off anywhere," said a cowboy.

"Then how come they call this place 'Stampede Mesa'?" said Abe.

"You tell us," Jake Wilson looked up from the cook pot he was scrubbing out with sand.

"Don't reckon the boss wants to hear it," muttered the old wrangler.

"Aw, go on, Abe," said Sherman. "You got them all curious now."

"Well, I was comin' through this country with an old man named Sawyer in 1891. Had a herd of about fifteen hundred head of steer. When he was drivin' across Dockum flats, six or seven miles over in that direction," Abe waved his arm toward the east, "about forty head of cows come bawlin' into his herd. And after 'em ran a farmer waving his arms hollerin', 'Cut my cattle out of that herd!'

"He was mighty upset 'cause his cattle was joinin' ours, and he saw all his stock being driven right off along with the big herd.

"Sawyer, a real tough character, hollered back 'Go to ____.' Well, on that drive he was short-handed; his cattle were already skinny from all the walkin', and he didn't want to gin 'em about any more.

"If you don't drop my cows out of that herd before dark I'll stampede 'em all," the farmer flung back in Sawyer's face as he watched that meager herd of his going off with ours.

"Vamoose!" Sawyer shouted, this time drawing his six-shooter and flourishing it like he was goin' to kill him on the spot. The farmer took off, and we thought that ended it.

"The cattle grazed peaceful-like on top of the mesa, and after dark they settled down pretty good. The cowboys stopped singing around the fire—somehow cattle sense that the men are their protectors—and we were all singin' that night to calm 'em and block out other noises. The herd was quiet as you please. I looked at them myself about ten o'clock. Since steep bluffs edged one side of the mesa we only had about half the usual number of nighthawks on watch duty.

"I went on to sleep thinking maybe I'd been silly about the whole thing, and I must have slept good for about two hours. Suddenly I woke up hearing cattle bawling and the sound of hooves. Within minutes we were up there on the mesa, but it was too late. A stampede spreads like a forest fire. That herd was crazy with fear. On level ground the boys can ride up beside the lead steers and mill them around to the rear until they finally wind the whole herd to a standstill with the leaders enclosed in the center of the circle. But on the south side of this mesa are the bluffs, and the cattle were starting to head toward them.

"True to his word, that farmer had slipped through the watch, and he was riding along in front of the herd on the north side waving a blanket in front of them like crazy and shooting off his gun. In a frenzy of fear the herd began stampeding in the opposite direction heading right for the bluff. We couldn't even hear Sawyer yelling orders at us over the sound of cattle bellowing.

"Two men rode out in front of the herd to try and circle them. In the crush they were carried right over the bluff with them. The herd was terrified. Of about fifteen hundred steers, we were only able to stop about three hundred from stampeding over the cliff.

"At sunrise you could tell by Sawyer's face he was dead tired but he was in a rage. He ordered our men to ride out after the farmer and bring him in, and they were back with him before noon.

"'Give me a lariat,' said he, and taking the length of rawhide he tied the fellow on his horse. Then, stripping off the dusty handkerchief from around his own neck, he blindfolded that horse, seized it by the bit, and began to back him toward the bluff. All of us went quiet while the man on the horse cried out for mercy. Sawyer's face only grew harder. He continued slowly leading that animal toward the edge. Then the horse's back feet slipped. I guess we near about held our breaths watching his front feet slide toward the brink. It was a bad sight to watch. As his mount pitched over the bluff the fellow gave a terrible scream. I'll never forget the sound of it. It got fainter and fainter 'til we couldn't hear it no more."

"And what is that supposed to mean?" snapped Grady Sherman.

"Nothin', 'cept it's why they call this place stampede mesa," said Abe.

The cowboys sat silent looking into the fire.

Abe rose and headed over toward the horses, taking them to a grassy patch a quarter of a mile away where he staked the bell mare, with a long rope, to a pin driven into the ground. The other horses bunched around her to go to sleep for the night. He had trained the remuda of horses so well that a rope pen was unnecessary.

Sherman stared after him with a hard look. During the first watch of the night the trail boss was always the one to stay with the herd watching for signs of nervousness and make certain they were settled. Meanwhile Abe checked his horses and decided to put Bessie on the first watch of the night. Bessie was a young horse, and he wanted the more experienced night horses on the later guards. The last watch was the hardest one and he had a mule for it. He had always held to the notion that a mule sees more clearly, smells more keenly and is a more cautious guard over a remuda than a horse.

Their men would need horses bad if anything happened during the night, he said to himself for he went along with the saying, "A man on foot is no man at all." But why was he thinking like that? Maybe Sherman was right pegging him as a superstitious old wrangler. The herd had settled down pretty fast and lay quietly on the ground, but somehow every time Abe heard a cow move he was alert. He just couldn't get the history of this place out of his mind. He heard a saddle creak and cursed to himself. One of the cowboys was dismounting too near the cattle, and the horse, shaking himself, rattled the empty saddle and stirrups. Not far from him someone struck a match. Both were little things a man could slip up and do without thinking. But nothing happened. Tonight the herd was quiet as a bunch of dead sheep. Abe fell asleep.

The next time he woke up was just before the watch changed for the second time. He stayed awake for a little while but the herd was still quiet. He was tired, and this time he fell into a dreamless, peaceful slumber.

When he woke again, the moon had set and the sky was dark as the black felt of a gunman's hat. The old wrangler stirred and sat up sleepily. Suddenly the herd was bellowing like thunder above him, and he was wide awake. The cattle were off and running.

"You, Jake—you, Mark—get out there and mill them," shouted Sherman.

Abe leaped on his horse. Other cowboys galloped up.

"Nobody else goes, boys," said Sherman warningly. "Just Mark and Jake."

Off they went while the others sat their mounts apprehensively. Two good men were more effective at circling a herd and bringing a stampede into a mill than a bunch of hard-riding cowboys yelling their heads off and shooting six-shooters.

The noise was like thunder that wouldn't stop. As Grady Sherman rode up beside Abe something went past them—a man on a horse! He seemed to be wafted along by the wind, and following it sailed a bay with a roan behind it, swept before the stampede. Horses and riders were headed straight for the bluff. Sherman looked around behind him to see the horns of a huge brute of a bull—skinny, long-legged, long-backed and long-tailed—overtaking him. The eyes of the trail boss were big as he watched, but the bull just passed right on through him.

The cattle seemed to see what was happening in their midst for they moved a little to one side, while behind the bull a pale horse drifted, blindfolded and with a rider tied astride its back. Even above the noisy bellowing, frightened sounds and pounding hoofs of the stampeding herd you could hear a man's voice crying out, and a long piercing wail.

Jake and Mark managed to keep their heads, milling the cattle into a circle cautious-like, winding the whole herd into a standstill, but they couldn't bed them down again that night. It took every man to hold them on the mesa.

Sherman rode up beside Abe exhausted, and they stared at each other. The face of the trail boss was white, and he looked years older.

"Did you see anything queer out there, Abe?"

Abe nodded. "I sure did. How about you?"

"That big bull and those steers—it was like they were floating all around us."

"Remember what happened in that stampede of '91? Steers went pitching right off the steep side of the mountain and hundreds of 'em died."

"Yep, I remember."

"I'd say this was their night to come back."

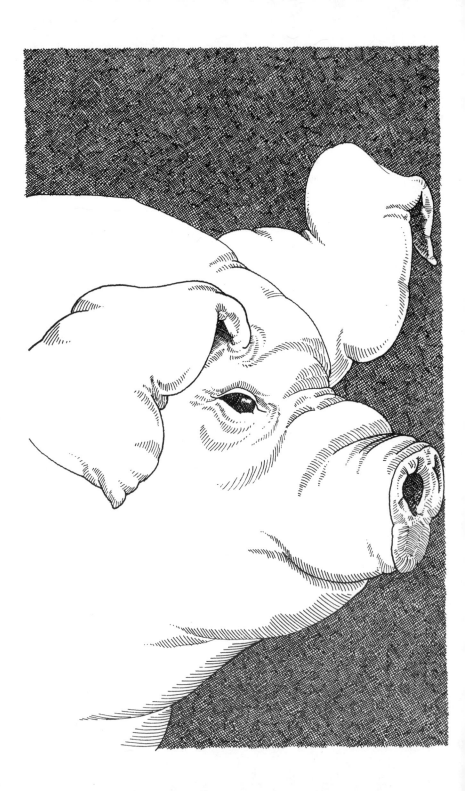

Alfie

WELL, OLD SUSIE had her pigs last night," said Jim Devlin, coming into the kitchen. "And every one of them alive." His wife Aileen had just put a big platter of eggs, scrapple, and potato pancakes on the table.

John, ten, and Mark, fourteen, began to help themselves. Only twelve-year-old Will stopped, serving spoon in midair.

"Is she doing all right?" said Mrs. Devlin.

"Fine."

"How many did she have, Dad?" spoke up Will.

"Fifteen—a large litter. The runt probably won't make it."

"There's a runt in every litter," announced Mark with an air of superiority.

"What do you know about it, Mark," said Will with a dark look at his older brother. "Why is that, Dad?"

"Don't know. I don't guess anybody does."

Will pushed back his chair excitedly. "I'm going out to look at them."

"Will! You're going to be late for school!" called his mother, but before she could finish Will was out the door.

"If he's late the teacher will punish him. Let him learn, Aileen," said her husband.

Jim Devlin, a tall, heavyset Irishman, and his wife, Aileen, a tiny, vivacious woman, had come over from Ireland in 1905, settling among other immigrants at Emmetsburg, Iowa. Then Devlin decided there would be more opportunity in the Des Moines area. Beginning all over again was not easy, but he purchased land, some still in timber, cleared most of it with Mark and Will's help, and planted corn and oats. Jim Devlin was most interested in raising a good grain crop, but like many farm families, they also owned a sow, a milk cow, and some chickens.

"Jim, you'd better go out and get him," said Aileen. "The way that boy loves animals, he'll be out there all day!"

"Guess you're right."

When his father reached the A-frame that sheltered the sow, there was Will down on the ground in the straw. He was holding the smallest pig.

"What're you doing, son?"

"Trying to see that it gets to nurse, Dad."

"That pig probably won't make it," said Devlin.

"It might," said Will hopefully. Hands supporting the warm little body, he was holding the tiny pink snout against the sow's nipple.

"I'm afraid not," said his father. "It doesn't weigh over two and a half pounds, son, and with that size litter it will be pushed aside most of the time. Off to school with you now."

That afternoon when he came home he tossed his books on his bed and headed straight for the mother sow. Pigs nurse every two hours, and again he helped the runt piglet compete with its fourteen sturdy brothers and sisters for the life-giving trickle of milk. The tiny animal sucked contentedly.

At school the next day he thought about the runt and what he could do to save it. It would starve to death, and what had it done to deserve such a fate? As soon as he got home he helped it nurse, and after supper he went out again. It was a girl, or rather a gilt, and he must decide on a name for it. Madelaine? Frances? Maureen? No, none of those would do. Finally he thought of Alfreida. He liked that. Henceforth the little gilt became "Alfie."

The following morning he was up at first light dressing hurriedly. He and his father almost bumped into each other in the upstairs hall as he came out of his bedroom leaving his younger brother asleep.

"Up so early?"

"I thought I would go out and see how the new litter is, Dad."

When his father arrived with the swill—ground-up grain, water and the "tankage" he purchased from the local packing plant, Will was already holding the runt, protecting her from the attempts of greedy siblings to push her out of the way. Alfie was feeding hungrily.

"So that's why you got up so early. Just don't let this interfere with your schoolwork, that's all."

"Dad, I've named her Alfie. It's short for Alfrieda."

"You have, have you?" He was pouring swill into the trough for the mother sow. Will hated the smell of the tankage, but his father insisted on using these animal by-products from the local packing plant. He said nobody knew why but hog raisers thought mixing tankage with the ground corn and oats grew stronger pigs. "Makes the sows give more milk, too," he would add when defending the practice.

Every day Alfie nursed greedily while Will pushed away her stronger and more aggressive brothers and sisters. She would positively gorge herself on milk for the three feedings a day during the week and four on Saturdays and Sundays that Will was at home to help her.

It showed. Alfie was growing fast and at the end of six weeks was ready for her first solid food of ground dry grain and tankage. Will would save the best swill for her, tipping the bucket on its side and wedging it between his legs so that she could walk right into it. Alfie devoured it eagerly and even began to stand her ground, refusing to be pushed away from the trough. Will was proud of her.

The October nights were cold and there had already been several light snowfalls when Will and his father put the pigs in the barn. Will fixed a special place for Alfie, changing the oat hay of her bedding often. He would head for the barn as soon as he came home from school, sometimes bringing her a carrot, which Alfie loved, and when the boy hugged her she would emit soft, affectionate little grunts and nuzzle him.

It was an especially hard winter in Des Moines that year. One Friday morning in December Will went out to see Alfie before school and found that she wouldn't eat. He changed her bedding, giving her fresh oat hay, and he didn't want to leave her that morning.

"She's just off her feed," said his father. "I wouldn't worry, son."

But after school when he hurried out to the barn to see Alfie he found her breathing labored and no affectionate grunts greeted him. Will ran back to the house.

"Dad, something's wrong with Alfie. Come out and take a look at her."

Carrying a lantern, for dusk comes early in December, he and his father walked across the snow covered ground to the barn. Alfie just lay there and when Jim Devlin looked at her and heard the rattle in her breathing his face became grave.

"I'm afraid it's pneumonia, Will."

"Will she get well?"

"Depends on how bad she has it."

"Dad, it's way down below zero. Don't we need to take her inside where it's warmer?"

"No place to put her, son."

"We could put her in my room beside my bed on a pallet. Please ...."

"I don't think your mother would like that, Will. I'm sorry. All you can do is keep her well-bedded and warm."

"I'll go back to the house and find an old blanket."

"Maybe you can get her to drink some weak swill—a little more water in it."

The boy was good with animals. Once it had been a motherless rabbit he had raised; another time he made a tiny splint for a bird with a broken wing. While he was in the house looking for something to keep Alfie warm, Will had an inspiration. In the small storeroom that led off his own bedroom stood a bathtub that his mother had been given by a family that moved back to Chicago. But her dream of indoor plumbing was one of many waiting for the time "when we're in tall clover," as his father described it.

While his father was absorbed in helping John with his numbers, Will, glad that it was a dark night without moonlight, managed to bring in some clean oat straw for the bottom of the tub. Then he went out the back door, a blanket under his arm, picked up all eighty pounds of Alfie, and wrapped her in it securely. His arms began to ache on the way to the house. He had to be careful that he would not be seen, so he had propped open one of the cellar doors so he could enter the house unobserved. The basement was the best route. Tenderly carrying his heavy bundle he walked ever so quietly until he reached the stairs. Finally he was in the storeroom placing Alfie on the clean straw and covering her with a warm blanket. He knew he would have to tell his father but that could wait until in the morning, and by then maybe, just maybe he would change his mind when he saw how cozy and warm Alfie was in the tub. It could help bring her through.

Sure enough, the next morning his father discovered the pig in the storeroom. He went in to tell his wife and was going to make Will take Alfie back to the barn when Mrs. Devlin intervened.

"Oh, Jim. Listen to that poor animal breathe. She's not doing a bit of harm in that tub," said his mother. "Leave her right where she is. I just wish there was something I could do." She turned to her husband. "Should I fix her a mustard plaster?"

Jim Devlin winced. "Don't do that to the animal. Just let her rest and keep warm. Jim can try her on food every so often. If she will take it from anyone, it will be him."

Jim Devlin stroked Alfie's head with its floppy ears.

"Keep trying her on swill but make it thinner, Will, and be sure to keep that straw clean."

Several days passed with Alfie's breathing still labored, but gradually she began to improve. Will brushed her gleaming white coat, but it was two weeks before he bathed her. By then she was getting restless in the tub, and his father thought she was well enough to go back to the barn. On warm days in March and April when Will walked around the barnyard Alfie would follow at his heels, and by the first of May it was warm enough for her to be put out to pasture. You would never know that the glossy, rotund gilt had once been the runt of the litter, and even Will's father was surprised.

"I think I could win a blue ribbon with her at the State Fair in August," said Will to his dad. "She looks like a real purebred—not a spot on that white coat of hers. What do you think?"

"I don't know, son. I'm in business to take care of this family, not raise show animals."

"But look at those floppy ears of hers, Dad. When Mr. Johnson from the fairgrounds was out here last week, I showed her to him, and he said he thought Alfie would win something because of those ears and because she's solid white and her weight is good." Alfie was nudging at his pocket, and Will pulled out the carrot he had brought her. She munched on it happily, nuzzling him now and then.

"How much does she weigh, Will?"

"Over three hundred pounds."

"Pretty good!" He patted Will on the back.

"She might even be a blue ribbon winner, Dad. See how glossy her coat is? I brush her every day."

"I know you do, Will." His father turned to go for more swill and Will saw him look tired.

"Wait—I'll get that for you, Dad," Will said.

Jim Devlin sat down on the barrel beside the well. He thought of the house—how it needed a new roof and a fresh coat of paint. There was always something and never enough money or time. Suddenly the big Irishman felt very discouraged, and he started back to the house. There were many Iowa farm homes like it—two-story white frame, a porch stretching all the way across the front, and wild pink roses in bloom around it. He loved that house. This time of year it sure looked pretty, and for a few minutes there was more of a spring in Devlin's step as he walked into the kitchen and gave Aileen a bear hug.

Then he remembered what he had to do.

"Aileen, I've got to tell Will about Alfie—that we will need to butcher her in two weeks to have enough cured meat for the family this fall."

"Oh, Jim!"

"That's the way it is on a farm, Aileen. It's the only one of the litter big enough."

"But he was hoping to show her at the next State Fair. That could mean lots of money."

"And are we to gamble on whether the pig wins?"

"She does look like a blue ribbon pig, Jim."

"We raise pigs for meat—not to show!"

"Oh, Dad!" They hadn't heard Will come in.

"Yes."

"You don't mean butcher Alfie?"

"Yes, I do."

"Not Alfie. One of the others. Please, Dad," Will begged.

"I'm sorry, son. You did a fine job of raising her, but she's the only one we've got that's right for butchering now so we will have food this fall. I know you wouldn't want the family to—"

But Will had turned and run from the room, the kitchen door slamming behind him.

"He's gone to the barn," said his father.

"Are you going after him?"

"No."

"He will miss his supper."

"He's got to learn."

They sat down and ate their meal in silence. Afterward Jim Devlin picked up an old newspaper and made a great show of reading every page while Aileen mended.

"Be nice to have one of those family cars folks are buying," he said, extending the paper with the advertisement for his wife to see.

"Perhaps when the day comes we don't have to butcher a boy's show pig for food we can think about that," said his wife, not raising her blonde head from the shirt she was mending.

"Honey, don't talk like that."

She held up the thread, and with quick motions bit it and knotted it, then compressed her lips.

Jim Devlin tried again. "That was mighty good rhubarb pie you made for supper."

Aileen gave a stiff little nod, and her husband gave up. Eight-thirty passed, nine o'clock, nine-thirty and still no Will. At ten o'clock Aileen said, "Don't you think you'd better go out and see about him?"

"I guess so."

A light snow was falling as Devlin walked to the barn.

"Will, Will!" There was no answer. He went over to Alfie's stall and holding the lantern high his eyes searched the enclosure until he saw Alfie's white coat gleaming in the dim light from the lantern, beside her Will's dark blue jacket. Will lay fast asleep, one arm flung across Alfie's neck, and from the streaks on his face he had evidently cried himself to sleep. His father took him back to the house.

The next two weeks were torture. Will was sure Alfie could have won a blue ribbon, but now he would never know. Over and over in his mind he told himself that it was his own fault. *If he hadn't taken such good care of her ... if he hadn't fattened her up so.* Alfie's fate was partly his fault.

The dreaded day arrived. After saying a tearful goodbye to the unsuspecting Alfie who responded with her usual soft gruntings and nuzzlings, Will went on to school.

When August and time for the State Fair arrived Will did not want to go with the rest of the family, but they finally persuaded him. As they arrived they stopped to watch the last group of swine being judged. Eight-foot pens lined one side of the arena and were numbered one through fifteen.

The judge was pacing around the arena. Then he pointed to a pen. "Go to pen #8," he was saying to an owner. The owner opened the cage door, tapped the rear of the animal and the pig walked obediently across the arena before the judge. Then he tapped the pig on the right side of the cheek to turn it to the left and on the left cheek to turn it back. It did not take long for the judge to scrutinize each entry. He would award the ribbon he thought the pig deserved.

Watching the judging made Will sadder than ever, and before it was over he got up to leave. His father signaled the rest of the family to follow.

"Next year, if that boy wants a pig to show, I'm going to give him a chance," said Devlin to his wife. "We'll make it somehow." She nodded, her eyes full.

Will was dragged reluctantly along with them to the livestock barns to look at the animals. They were walking from pen to pen commenting on the prize winners when Jim Devlin stopped in front of one of them and gasped.

At that moment ten-year-old John started shouting, "Look! Look, everybody. It's Will's pig!"

Will, who had lagged behind, cried out, "Shut up! I hate you, John!"

But the whole family had stopped in front of one of the pens, and Jim Devlin reached out for his son's arm pulling him over in front of it. It was the last pen on the last row. "Wait a minute. Look at this, Will." In the pen was a Chester white sow, and it was Alfie. The whole family recognized her. The card on the gate read *Alfie—Will Devlin, Des Moines, Iowa.* Beside the card was a blue ribbon.

After his initial surprise Devlin's next thought was that someone was playing a very ugly trick. It just couldn't be Alfie for he knew what had become of Alfie.

Together they went and talked to an official of the livestock board. He ran his finger down the list checking every entry in the swine category.

"Sorry. There's no sow named Alfie submitted by a Will Devlin."

The Devlins convinced him to come back with them to the livestock barn. When they reached the barn the pen on the last row was empty. Nor was there any card or blue ribbon. The official frowned, stared at them as if they were all insane, and left without a word. Jim Devlin could hardly look at his son—if ever a grown man felt like crying, he did. Turning, he was about to try to mumble something comforting, then stopped himself.

There stood his son in front of the empty pen, his face alight with happiness for the first time in weeks. Will knew exactly what had happened.

Alfie had made it to the State Fair, and she had won her blue ribbon.

OMENS AND PREDATORS

The Owl Omen

"WE'VE DONE PRETTY WELL tonight. A possum for you, a possum for me," said Tom Simmons as he and his friend rode along on horseback.

"Well, I told my brother-in-law in Hot Springs that we were going hunting, and he asked if I'd get a possum for him. He'll be disappointed," said Jody Johnson.

"Anything to prevent him from going himself?"

"No, but I owe him a favor. He helped me get my stable built."

"You're talking about your wife's brother, Arvin? Didn't you help him?"

"You're right, I did. But he says these woods are dangerous at night, and he doesn't want to be out here."

"Some fellows are afraid of their own shadow."

"Nobody would ever say that of you, Tom. When you were growing up, if there was a fight you were usually in the thick of it."

"Guess I'm hot-tempered like my granddaddy Simmons."

"The one that was the gold miner?"

"Yep."

"I heard he killed a man out in California. Self-defense?"

"Oh, he had good reason. The man was insulting his wife."

"I'd want to shoot a man for insulting Ellie, but I wouldn't do it," said Jodie in some surprise.

"You mean you'd back down—let him get away with it? Not me."

"Times were probably different then."

"No place for cowards in the gold mining region. Not if you were going to get rich," added Tom, who always had a full wallet although no one quite knew how he made all his money.

The pair rode silently for awhile.

Then Jody said, "This is a pretty lonely road we're taking back to town."

"All roads seem lonely at night."

"Don't we sometimes take another trail not so heavily wooded?"

"Depends on where we're coming from or going to," Tom said noncommittally. Jody felt a surge of irritation.

Tom must have noticed his silence for he said a few minutes later, "Think Franklin Delano Roosevelt's WPA is ever going to help Arkansas?"

"It's sure better than doing nothing or standing in line for food," replied Jody. The bushes rustled and his horse shied.

"Must have heard some critter in the brush nearby," said Tom, and on they went.

"We're hunting pretty far from home," said Jody, looking around him a little nervously, not quite sure where they were. "It's easy to lose track of your landmarks when the hunting's good."

"Yep. You could see those possums in the moonlight plain as could be."

"It's dark out here now. What happened to that moon?"

"Slipped just behind the clouds."

A little later pale beams of moonlight, poking through cloud cover, illuminating the trail intermittently. Suddenly there was a rustle at the horses' feet that frightened both animals.

"What in tarnation was that?" Simmons said irritably. "Easy boy, easy," he said patting the neck of his large bay. "Must be a weasel out hunting. The sound of the horses on the trail scared it."

The moon came out, defining the shape of the trees and outlining the trail ahead.

"Heard the Dinner Bell Diner is going to close?" asked Jody.

"Yep. Not enough business through the week anymore. Depression, I guess. The boys drop in there for a nickel cup of coffee but they eat to home."

"I'll miss—"

Suddenly Jody was interrupted by a deep booming sound, and a rabbit that had heard it too dashed across the trail in front of their horses.

"What was that noise, Tom?"

"I don't know."

Then came another sound altogether that could only be described as a long agonized moan, and a great horned owl fluttered down just in front of the horses' feet. The two horses reared and pawed the air, and the owl flew from the ground straight up over their heads. Jody's mount shied off the road into the scrub oaks and pines, Jody grasping the limbs and holding them back from the mare's face as he guided her back to the road, talking to her and patting her comfortingly.

"What's that on your mare's neck?" asked Tom.

"Good Lord! It must be blood!"

"No. I don't think it's blood. Let's see your hands, Jody. Berry juice—that's all it is."

"Sure feels sticky. Ugh." Jody wiped his hands on his handkerchief and bent down trying to wipe the red liquid from his horse's neck.

As they cantered on they heard a weird chorus of catlike noises followed by wild peals of laughter. Down swooped the horned owl again; they could see its great wingspread plainly in the moonlight.

"Whew! Big fellow, isn't he?"

"Probably has a nest near us," said Tom.

There was another flutter of wings and the immense body hurtled past, yellow eyes blazing at them from the midst of a dead white face.

"That Great Horned Owl must be out hunting. It will go after jackrabbits or other owls," said Simmons, unruffled. "I didn't know there were any around here."

"I don't like it," said Jody nervously. "The Indians were superstitious about Great Horned Owls and dreaded the sight of one of them."

"You superstitious like redskins?" said Tom.

"No. I'm just telling you, Tom, that some believe that a spirit may appear in the form of a bird as a warning. I've heard that many woods are haunted by spectral birds."

"Well, I'll be!" Simmons replied in disgust.

With another swoop the enormous owl came plummeting down in front of them almost at their feet.

"That bird is trying to tell us something," persisted Jody Johnson.

"*Who, who, who* could talk like such a fool!" Tom's mocking hoots were almost as loud as the owl's.

"You don't believe that an event can happen to warn you, Tom? It can. Once I was on my way home to get my gun because a stranger had cheated me in a card game. I was going to go back to the saloon with my gun under my arm to confront him when one of the strongest winds I've ever seen came up and a tree fell across a place in the road just a few yards ahead of me. If I had been a minute sooner it would have crushed me."

"And you didn't go ahead and get the guy?"

"No siree. That tree almost striking me made me think, and when I got home I put the gun back up over the fireplace. Later I heard that fellow who cheated me had a bad name. Bartender said he'd killed two men and got off for it."

"You might have picked him off."

"And I might not have."

"You're loco, Jody. And that owl's not telling me a thing."

Tom's words were followed by loud, inhuman laughter as if the owl was deriding him. Both men were jittery. After the last shrieks of mirth faded they heard a series of eerie moans.

"Sounds like somebody's being murdered!" Tom said in an awed voice.

Again and again the owl swooped down at their horses' feet while both horses whinnied with fright and attempted to bolt. Jody's hands were sweating as he reined in his mare.

"We ought to take another road," he said, turning to Tom. "Let's take the one that branches off at the fork."

"You're crazy!"

"No. That bird is an omen," said Jody. He had always heard that an owl was sensitive to evil influences, and that the moaning of the bird was a sign of approaching death. By now they had reached the fork and the old road led off to the left.

"This road goes to my place, too," said Jody.

"It's at least five miles out of your way. Omens! You superstitious fool!"

"Call me whatever you want," said Jody.

The upshot of it was that the two parted, agreeing to meet about ten o'clock the next morning at Ward's Store where they both traded. Jody rode off. Several times, lulled by the rhythmic canter of his horse, he was on the verge of falling asleep in the saddle. He was tempted to slump over and doze, but his horse was not familiar with this road home. Each time his eyes closed and his chin began to drop upon his chest, he somehow managed to jerk upright without falling out of the saddle. Even in his fringed leather coat he felt the piercing cold of the night.

It was two in the morning when he finally reached home and dropped into bed, bone-tired. Jody realized that he had ridden his mare much further than if he had accompanied his friend on the other road. Now that he was safe and warm at home he thought maybe he really was a fool.

Next morning he woke to the fragrance of coffee and bacon frying and when his wife put some hoe cake in front of him he gave her a quick hug.

"I didn't even hear you when you came in," said Ellie. "It must have been mighty late. You got a possum, didn't you?"

"Yes. A fat one."

"I'll barbecue it and fix up some persimmon pudding to go with it."

"Makes my mouth water just to think about it."

"Never known you to be that late. Anything happen, Jody?"

Jody's face flushed.

"Oh, we just had to run the possum some."

"Run them?" she repeated, "You mean the way they used to shoot down buffalo years ago?" She looked at him doubtfully.

Jodie had hoped to avoid telling her the reason he had been so late but saw he couldn't. Shamefacedly he told her how he and Tom had disagreed about which road to take coming home, and how he had decided to take the long way.

"But why, Jody?"

"I heard an owl scream and I—"

"An owl? You rode all that extra distance because of an owl?" she said in astonishment.

Jodie could feel his face reddening from the roots of his strawberry blond hair clear down to his collar. "Yes, I did. Now, listen to me."

He described how the huge eagle owl had repeatedly swooped down in front of them right at their horses' feet.

"Sometimes that owl would utter a deep booming sound you could hear all through the woods—loud, echoing. Then we would hear an outburst of noises just like a cat would make, and that was followed by the eeriest moaning I ever heard. Ellie, it was enough to make your flesh crawl."

She nodded, not looking at him. When he had finished telling her about it he went outdoors to feed the livestock, doing everything in slow motion, tired from lack of sleep the night before. Embarrassed about the whole incident, he squirmed at the thought of what jokes Tom would make about it at the store and the teasing. Taking out of his pocket the gold timepiece that had been his father's, he flicked open the elaborate engraved cover with his fingernail—five minutes before ten. He was going to be late.

It was ten-thirty when he pulled up before Ward's Store. The first horse he saw tethered out in front was Tom's, and he knew they must all be inside laughing, for Tom had a way with words and could make something comical out of anything when he wanted to. Right then Jody could have turned around and driven somewhere else to get his supplies, but he braced himself and walked in. Before he was halfway there, Smith, Pyeatt, Williams and Rector were all talking at once.

"Jody. Thought you weren't going to make it this morning. Where's your pardner?"

"Isn't he here? His horse is tethered outside."

"Bill tethered it. When he came in this morning he saw Tom's horse grazing out there with no saddle, but we haven't seen hide nor hair of Tom."

One of the other men piped up, "Yeah. If it had been some other fellow I'd say as how he was thrown, and that the horse went off and left him where he lay, but I can't see that happening to Tom. He's too good a rider."

"I went by his house to see if he wanted to ride over to the store with me," interrupted Rector. "His wife said he never came home last night."

"We better start looking for him. A man's horse don't just wander up without something is bad wrong," said Barnaby Williams, a deputy sheriff, "specially Tom Simmons." You could see he didn't care too much for Tom.

Jody suddenly came out of his state of shock.

"He and I went hunting last night. A pretty good piece from town, we said goodbye, and I took another way home. We agreed to meet here at Ward's this morning."

"You lead the way, Jody. Let's see if we can find him."

The road looked different to Jody in the sunlight from the way it had in the dark the night before. The brush didn't seem as thick nor the woods as menacing.

"I come this way at night pretty often," said Oliver Smith. "Folks are always saying that a lot of mischief goes on out here—people robbed—but nobody ever gave me any trouble."

"Seen any owls along here?"

"No. Not enough large animals left for the big ones to feed on nowadays," said Smith, "but maybe a few little ones are left." He stared at Jody curiously. "Why?"

"Just wondered. I thought I heard one last night."

"I doubt that, but even if you did, they won't get close. They're scared of people."

They didn't have far to go.

"Wait a minute, boys. Hold your horses," said the young deputy sheriff. He got down from his horse and examined some brush that looked as if it had been trampled. Then, parting it with his hands, the men heard him gasp, and Jody was at his side. Tom's body lay face down, as if it had been thrown there like a rag doll. The back of his head, all bloodied, had been dealt a tremendous blow. When they turned him over his eyes were open wide with an expression of surprise, and beside him was his empty wallet.

"If it hadn't been for that owl ..." mumbled Jody.

"What do you mean owl, Jody?" said sheriff's deputy, Barnaby Williams. "Tom was murdered by a robber for whatever he had on him."

"Tom Simmons was never afraid of anything," said someone.

"Well, mebbe he shoulda been," said the deputy, spitting tobacco juice, and he put his jacket over the face of the body.

As Jody rode home late that afternoon he heard the hoot of an owl, and it was not yet dark. Come to think about it he had never seen an owl in these parts before last night. Tom Simmons, alive yesterday afternoon, was now dead at Coleman's Funeral Parlor, and he, Jody, was lucky to be alive. Or was it something more than just luck?

The sound came again—fainter now—and from much farther off in the distance. It was almost like a farewell.

Who-o-o, who-o-o, who-o-o-o-o.

He shivered.

Prowler of the Cumberlands

THE CREATURE IN THE CAVE raised its head and listened intently. Hearing nothing, he began to drink from the spring—long, thirsty drafts of fresh, cool water. The lapping sound was heard by only a few wakeful and cautiously hidden denizens of the forest. It was almost midnight. Somewhere in the valley the barking of dogs could be heard followed by a chorus of howls, and then in the distance a man's shout broke the stillness. The creature was instantly alert. Lifting its head it bared its teeth in a ferocious snarl and sniffed the breeze.

Then, padding swiftly and silently out of the cave, its long sinuous body disappeared in the forest of oak, pine, and hickory from whence it had come.

Through the beautiful Sequatchie Valley between Crossville, Tennessee, and Bridegeport, Alabama, flows the Sequatchie River, emerald green and clear, mirroring the shadows of the high Cumberland mountains. Small iron ore producing communities are strung like beads beside it, among them the town of Sequatchie. Though mining, corn, and wheat crops supported the townspeople, the chief industry was the handle factory. As one might suppose, its employees made all sorts of tool handles, and although other factories would close in the years to come, the need for handles would last forever.

Few events marred the tranquility of Sequatchie Valley during these days of the early nineteen hundreds, unless we count the untimely visits of revenuers, dog fights, or the occasional resurgence of a feud among old settlers.

The schoolmaster Robert Wheeler was a widower with a little girl. Brought ashore by chance on the emerald waters of the river, he stayed on to enjoy a quiet, bucolic life of reading, fishing, hunting, and the companionship of neighbors. In time he became engaged to the daughter of one of the managers of the handle factory. But a Virginian himself, he never forgot that this was wilderness country, an outpost between savagery and civilization, and not many decades ago inhabited by Indians.

In March of 1908 Wheeler was out hunting shortly before midnight when his two dogs—thirty or forty yards ahead of him—started barking. Treed a possum he guessed, but suddenly their frenzied barking ceased. A cloud swathed the moon, and his dogs disappeared from sight. He called to them, and they answered, a chorus of yips and howls rising in the crisp night air.

They must have been following a scent, for their voices floated back to him from the direction of the path to Blowing Spring, and so, half running, he forced his way toward the sound as fast as the thick underbrush permitted. At night animals visited the spring to drink. Were the dogs on the trail of one of them? Suddenly the clouds parted, the moon shone through, and his feet easily found the well-trodden way to the spring. Rounding a curve he saw a surprising sight. There was his hunting dog, Blackie—usually eager, aggressive—crouched on the ground trembling, and Duke, an enormous mixed breed animal with some German shepherd in him, bravely taking his stand beside her, emitting throaty, menacing growls. But at what? Upon his approach the animal—if it was an animal—must have heard him and fled, but despite his pats and encouragement neither dog wanted to pursue their prey further. Something must have spooked them. He could feel their fear, but could not imagine its source, for there was no animal in these woods Duke and Blackie wouldn't tackle.

After looking around the area and finding nothing, Wheeler headed home. Unfortunately the incident dredged up a long submerged memory. Years ago, he had gone hunting with his father and younger brother, Edgar. Too young to be trusted as yet with a shotgun, Edgar had ventured ahead of them, and Robert heard him cry out. Robert started running until he saw Edgar standing in a clearing, face to face with an enormous black bear. The animal couldn't have been more than twenty feet away from his brother. Paralyzed by fear, Robert was unable to move.

Then the branches rustled near him, and his father, gun raised, began shooting. The bear took several lumbering steps toward the boy. His father stepped out into the clearing, still firing. Faltering, the animal dropped to the ground no more than five feet short of Edgar. Robert was in the clearing himself by then but could not meet his father's gaze.

Even now he blushed with shame at the memory of how he had failed his younger brother—and himself. His father, known for his hunting prowess, had never spoken a word of blame, but in later years it was Edgar, full of bravado, who accompanied his father on hunting trips and whose exploits he related.

Ever since he had moved to the valley, Wheeler had heard from Tennessee old-timers that the Cumberland Mountains had been infested with wolves, panthers, and all sorts of wild beasts until Civil War days. In fact, it was impossible to raise livestock in the area. But that was almost fifty years ago. As time passed, the ancient prowlers of the Cumberlands dwindled and stock raisers could pasture their cattle with a peaceful mind.

The Monday after Wheeler had gone hunting, he made a shopping trip to South Pittsburgh. Eating lunch in the Lowman Hotel, he began to scan a copy of the local paper. According to *The South Pittsburgh Hustler,* a strange creature had been seen on the streets the night before near Sartain's Drugstore and the First National Bank building. Wheeler's friend, Robert Potter, a Civil War veteran with a reputation for having been a hero, wandered in. Over a drink Potter told him that he was there himself, and that fifty shots had been fired at the creature but it had escaped unwounded!

And it wasn't because of poor marksmanship either, thought Wheeler wryly, because in the free-for-all fights common to that section of the valley, the peaceful inhabitants usually managed to kill two or three of their fellow townsmen and wound as many more with only half that amount of gunplay.

Wheeler had been here ten years now teaching school. His daughter, Catherine, was just reaching the age when she took pride in keeping house for him, seizing every opportunity to show him ways she could improve on his makeshift masculine methods. On March 12, she would be twelve years old.

Sometimes he thought of taking her back east because Sequatchie, Tennessee, though no longer regarded as "the West," was still frontier country and did not have the advantages of Virginia. There was not even any electricity out here yet. But if he went back, he would wait until after he and Laura were married. Seeing Laura's lovely dark head next to Catherine's as they worked doing his daughter's homework by the light of a kerosene lamp, he was amazed by their resemblance to each other. Many people would probably assume she was the girl's natural mother.

As Wheeler left South Pittsburgh for Sequatchie, he remembered that he and Cathy needed water at home. He must see about it when he returned. They had plenty of water to bathe in but were running low on drinking water. When he returned, he would go to the cave at Blowing Spring where the townspeople filled their water buckets. Looking at his gold watch, he realized he would not be home until shortly before dusk. Catherine would want to go with him. Since his conversation at the hotel with Potter, he thought it better not to visit the spring at dusk but postpone the trip until tomorrow.

He had just returned to Sequatchie when he met Frank Fletcher and stopped to greet. him. Fletcher, a tall, rangy fellow, quick to smile and usually ready with a joke, lived over at Victoria. Today he had a startling piece of news. Some unknown animal had visited Victoria and left a trail of terror behind it, killing as many as twenty-five dogs on a single visit and neatly slitting the throat of each. No one knew what sort of animal had done this, but someone had dubbed it "The Marauder."

The animal's visits did not seem to last over thirty minutes and often took place just after dusk. He thought about how afraid his two dogs had been a few nights before and wondered whether the marauder had anything to do with it. It was unlikely but he decided to shut them up that night.

Fletcher had still more to tell.

"You know Lula Lamb. Did you hear about her?"

Wheeler knew her by sight. "What about Lula?"

Fletcher pushed the local paper toward him. "Here. Read it yourself."

"Strange Animal Still Annoying Night Travelers," read the March 1 newspaper headline with a dateline of Victoria, and he read the story that followed with interest.

> Miss Lula Lamb, a few days ago, was followed by some animal while on her way to the store. It was about dusk when she noticed something following her. She screamed and ran till she reached a store, when the storekeeper, hearing her cries, came out to find the cause, and the animal disappeared.

Bob Wheeler went on to the item below.

> Mrs. Nancy Copeland, who lives in English Cove on the mountain above Whitwell, also had a terrifying experience with the strange animal who had the temerity to attack her. She had returned to her

home from a visit to the family of Hugh Morrison, when she noticed something beneath the porch of her house. She tried to get into the house but was attacked by something which sprang at her, almost knocking her down. She caught hold of the banisters of the porch, which saved her from falling, and then managed to get into the house.

Whatever it is, the animal is keeping people indoors at night, and children are so scared they're afraid to go to bed.

"That's bad enough," said Fletcher, "but did you hear about Mandy Ashburn's scare?"

"Not a thing."

"She was climbing up into the loft of her barn one day last week and scared out some big animal which jumped the fence and made off. She didn't get a close look at it, but said it was yellow and had a large, bushy tail."

"What in the world!" exclaimed Wheeler.

"Your guess is as good as mine. Up on the mountain above Whitwell, Pat Morrison was coming back from work about dusk. He saw a strange animal in the road, shouted at it and the critter snarled at him before taking off."

"Doesn't sound good, does it?" said Wheeler, thinking of his dogs and their puzzling behavior.

"No. It sure doesn't. The paper ran another story saying that the Marauder was still rampant—guess 'rampant' means ready to go on more rampages. I don't like it myself."

"What do you think it is, Frank?" asked Wheeler curiously.

Fletcher looked around him. "I probably shouldn't say this to someone city educated like you, Bob, and a schoolteacher, too." He paused, waiting until after a young lady had passed them, and then he looked hard at his friend as if almost daring him to treat what he was going to say as a joke.

"There are some who say it's the ghost of one of the ancient prowlers."

Wheeler could feel the hair prickling on the back of his neck.

"Wait a minute, Frank. A ghost isn't able to kill anything, and that goes for the ghost even of a wolf or a panther."

"All right. I didn't think you'd go for the idea, but this critter's been reported seen near Pikeville and thirty minutes later in South Pittsburgh. You realize they're fifty miles from each other!"

"Then it's not the same animal, Frank," said Wheeler. "Use your head!"

"Well, why are these reports turning up from all over the place when they never have before?"

"What does this animal look like?"

"Now that's a good one! They all seem to see something different," Fletcher admitted a little sheepishly. "One fellow said he saw a huge police dog with a bushy tail. Another said the color of the critter was yellowish. And a woman claimed that it traveled so fast the only impression she got was of a blue streak."

"You sure it all doesn't come from too much white lightning?" asked the schoolmaster with a smile.

"All right, Bob. Listen to this. A posse sent out after it said they had it surrounded in an open field but when they closed in upon it, the creature vanished." He paused, waiting for the full effect of his words to sink in.

"What are the police doing about it?" asked Robert.

"I hear they imported a pack of cat hounds and were out last night swearing they would catch the creature. After striking its trail on the mountain about South Pittsburgh, a lively race began. But when the dogs thought they were going to catch it, the animal turned on them and killed the leaders while the rest ran trembling with their tails between their legs."

"Whew!" said Wheeler, thinking once more about Duke and Blackie's behavior. "How about in the town of Sequatchie? Has it been here?"

"Some children were fishing in the river the other day and the animal approached them. Since then most parents haven't let their children out after five o'clock, and business places are talking about closing promptly at six. You'd better warn Catherine."

"Perhaps I had at that," said Wheeler. He looked at his watch. Four o'clock. He had told Catherine they would take his wheelbarrow and go to the spring for water this afternoon.

"By the way, I'm going out with a posse tonight to see if we can run it down. Want to join us?"

Bob Wheeler hesitated. "When you know what kind of varmint you're looking for, I'll go," said he and then more seriously, "Cathy and I plan to be—well—out for awhile tonight."

"I can't imagine where," said Fletcher with a grin.

But when Wheeler reached the house and called his young daughter there was no answer. Walking out on the back porch he saw that a small wagon he had bought for hauling things was gone. So were the water buckets. For a moment he felt sick, and then he told himself how crazy he was. Fletcher's talk was causing him to be an imaginative fool! She had probably just started toward the spring, and he could catch up with her before she reached it. He had told Catherine many a time that he didn't want her going alone, but she was always stubborn—bent on proving she could do anything. Probably grown impatient for him to get home.

He hurried across the clearing and entered the woods, restraining his desire to run, so he wouldn't miss the short cut that led to the Blowing Spring trail. Some ten minutes passed and he was growing warm despite the March weather. Looking at his watch he saw that it was five o'clock. The sun was setting. Where was she! She was further ahead than he had supposed, and he began to grow angry. Finally he saw her up ahead of him on the trail. She appeared to be pulling the cart along happily and all was well. He was an idiot to listen to all that fool talk, he thought to himself.

Suddenly, he was startled to see her standing stock still in the middle of the path. He hurried quietly up behind her, started to call out and then stopped himself.

Something was crouching before her—the largest panther he had ever seen. He felt the perspiration break out on his face and his legs were trembling. The animal was ready to spring. And then he reached for a rock and hurled it with all his strength. It struck the powerful body with a thud. Catherine turned and saw him, and he put his finger to his lips to warn her to be quiet. It might make a difference. Surprised by the rock, the huge cat turned his head to see where it had come from and hesitated. Then it reared up on its hind legs, and by the light of the moon Wheeler saw that it was a yellowish color and taller than a man. He had no weapon with him, and for a few seconds the players in the tableau stood immobile.

But Wheeler was seeing another terrifying moment. He was watching a bear rather than a panther and the animal was about to attack his brother. Suddenly he was drained of any strength. He watched the animal recover itself and take a step toward the girl, teeth bared in a vicious snarl.

Helpless, without a gun or even a club to strike with, Robert

Wheeler used the only weapon he had—his own body—at the same time shouting, "Run, Cathy. Run!"

He lunged straight at the panther, his head striking the midsection with all the weight of his six-foot frame behind it. He knew that any second he would feel sharp teeth tearing at his head and face, but his daughter would have a chance. He hoped she would take it.

To his amazement the animal seemed to give way before him and with lightning-like rapidity it melted into the woods.

"Dad, is it really gone?" his daughter cried, hugging him.

"Yes. It's gone," said Wheeler weakly.

"Are you hurt?"

"I don't believe so," he said, and the words that echoed through his head were Fletcher's: *Some people think it's the ghost of one of the prowlers ... one of the ancient prowlers.* Were there really such things?

Terribly shaken, his breath still coming quickly, he stooped to examine the path where the panther had stood a few seconds before. There were no footprints.

"Dad, I can't believe you're all right," said Cathy, hugging him. "You're the bravest man in the world!"

Maybe I am, thought Wheeler, and he liked the feeling. He still didn't know just what had happened, but his inner picture of Edgar and the bear was gone. It had fled in the face of his encounter with one of the "ancient prowlers."

The Plat-eye

FORTY MILES SOUTH OF CHARLESTON, embraced by two tidal rivers, there is a magic island. Its name is Edisto. An air of unfathomable mystery lies beneath the apparently normal scene of beach houses and tourist activities. The Spanish moss surrounds the live oaks like filmy gray specters, and in the old houses, stories of supernatural presences abound.

Among the stories woven into the rich fabric of the South Carolina island lore is that of a vicious supernatural creature called the plat-eye. Believed to be the spirit of a dead person, the plat-eye is able to take on animal form and change its shape rapidly from one beast to another. It guards valuables that families concealed in Civil War days, and it also stands vigil over buried pirate treasures. Our story centers around two plat-eye encounters.

The first befell Daisy Scott Brown, who lives on Edisto today, and the second happened to a man in the 1930s. His story will long be remembered, although no one is sure of his name. For the sake of convenience, we shall call him Will McClellan.

Now it wasn't that Will had not heard of how dangerous a plat-eye can be, for he had listened wide-eyed to stories about them since childhood. But when his poverty was more than he could bear, Will grew desperate—desperate enough to go hunting for a plat-eye's treasure.

When Will was a child, his granddaddy had told him how to go about it, and he remembered the old man's instructions word for word. "When you hear a rattling loud in the middle of the night deep in Murray Wood, that's the noise of a plat-eye rubbing itself against a tree trying to loose his chain. Go toward it. Where the rattling's the loudest, look for the oldest tree. Then, digee, digee, dig. There's treasure there."

One night, just after midnight, Will woke. Deep in Murray Wood he had heard the metallic clink of a chain, and he remembered his grandfather's words. Jerking on his clothes, Will made up a little song which he sang softly over and over.

> *"Fill up my house with groceries,*
> *Put a good dress on my wife's back,*
> *Throw a five dollar bill in the collection plate,*
> *The treasure I have found!"*

The stars were like lighted matches flaring and disappearing in an overcast sky. Fog slipped furtively through the woods, slithered around the tree trunks, and crouched in the low places. He looked about him nervously. Except for the chorus of cicadas and the sound of small night creatures, most of the varmints were fast asleep.

Will was on Hess Road before the moon showed herself. Not far from the direction where he was sure he'd heard the chain rattle, the road passed through the darkest, loneliest part of the forest, but he was too preoccupied to be frightened. Following the wagon track, he watched on his left and he watched on his right until finally there it was, the tree that had to be *the one*.

Sidling around it once, twice, three times, Will paused and leaned on his spade, listening. Then he drew a deep breath to steady his nerves. If he didn't hear anything, if he didn't see anything, if he could keep his hands from trembling, he would dig. He waited. Finally he was sure he was alone, and he started toward the tree ready to lead off with a vigorous thrust of the shovel. He had taken three steps toward it when he saw a dog rise right up out of the ground and rush at him. It was inches away from his legs and close enough to get a good look at. He saw a chewed-off ear, a spine sagging like it was broken in two, and three legs in the rear.

"It's a plat-eye! Plat-eye sure's you're born!" he exclaimed under his breath, and he stopped dead in his tracks.

Then the dog faded and in its place Will saw a huge, fiery-eyed black calf, so malevolent looking he shut his eyes tight. Every hair on his head stood straight up with shock. Backing away, he stumbled and fell to the ground struck senseless by fright. He didn't know how long he lay there on his back in the mud, but when he came to he thought maybe God hadn't meant for him to have this treasure after all.

Then, remembering his needy family, Will forced himself to get up. He dashed at the tree like crazy. Suddenly the ground burst open at his feet, and rising out of it he saw a monstrous, bloodthirsty hog—sharp teeth jabbing straight out, body scaly all over like alligator skin—the most awful looking thing Will had ever seen.

Wheeling around, he tried to escape but it was too late. It was coming right at him! The hog plunged between his legs, hurling him face-down into the stinking mire of the swamp and burying him so deep he could hardly draw breath. For over four hours Will lay there semi-conscious.

Wherever his skin was bare he could feel tiny rat's feet scampering over him and snakes wriggling across his flesh. Mercifully he fainted. When Will McClellan came to, the stars had vanished, a rooster was crowing, and it was morning. He had lain in the mire of the swamp all night, and where was all the money?

Later McClellan told his wife, "That treasure is still underground, and there I was on top of it sicker than a dog that's eaten spoiled mullet."

He shook his head with the air of one to whom knowledge has come too late and said, "Plat-eyes just tangle you up, make you forget your God."

Everyone on the island heard about Will's search for treasure for years to come.

It was different with Daisy. A hard-working girl with a job, it never entered her head to search for buried treasure. If she had ever harbored any such thoughts, the strange stories told on summer nights beneath the pulsating Spanish moss would have dissuaded her.

When Daisy Scott Brown was growing up on Edisto she walked through the woods on her way to school in the morning and back through them on her way home every afternoon. Beneath the canopy of live oaks, all twisted into weird shapes by the sea wind, it was always twilight.

Daisy's parents had both passed on years ago, and to her had fallen the duties of raising the younger children. A tall, well-built young woman, she made just enough money from housecleaning to take care of their needs, shopping rummage sales to buy coats and shoes for her brother and sister to wear in the fall and shorts and sneakers in the spring. They lived happily with one of her aunts near the road leading to Edisto Beach. Their house was weathered to a silvery hue, and across the sandy yard tall pines and ancient oaks threw long shadows from the edge of the woods.

Daisy always knew that those woods were inhabited by the ghosts of animals. She had seen them as a child crouching near the foot of the large trees, vaulting across her path or peering at her from behind the foliage with dark, limpid eyes. Her elders told stories explaining how they got there.

"People would bury treasure at the foot of a tree and kill an animal so's its ghost would guard it," they said, nodding, sagely. "The ghosts of little animals are harmless, but now you take plat-eyes—they're different. They'll lead you into danger, lose you in the swamps, steal your wits, and sometimes even leave you alone to die. Stay away from them."

Daisy knew they were often seen when someone died, and the death of a human could bring forth a spirit like this with the power to change itself at will. Some said it could take the form of a large five-legged calf, others a hunched-back yellow dog. The plat-eye stayed near treasure sites and would divert attention from the spot it guarded by a frenzied whirling, like a beast possessed by devils.

Sometimes, as Daisy nervously hurried her brother and sister along the trail through the twilight woods, she would see peering eyes and shadowy shapes, but not a plat-eye. She hoped she never would. She'd grown up knowing that in the past folks hid their valuables in the woods and set a plat-eye to watch over them. If anyone was foolish enough to go searching later, the plat-eye would rise straight up in the air out of nowhere and scare the thief to death.

But she really didn't worry about seeing them. She'd had her own supernatural experiences working at the big houses on the island. Cooking and cleaning, she'd seen apparitions in the fine old homes and even around the yards. One home had been the scene of a murder, and pitching headlong down the stairs, the dying man had spattered blood all over the wall. With much scrubbing she tried to wash it away, and for awhile the discoloration disappeared, but the outline would always return, growing darker and darker.

"The folks living in that house never could get paint to cover those stains for long," recalled Daisy, "and while I worked there, that same wall had to be repainted again."

Daisy lived almost within a shell's toss of the ocean.

"I listen to the surf some nights when it's a soft song, lulling me to sleep. Other nights I can't sleep because of the sound of the waves crashing on the beach—maybe the sign of a hurricane on the way."

A devout woman, she attended the A.M.E. Zion Church each Sunday. During the week she cooked at a small restaurant, and most of her days followed a peaceful routine except for that one day she will never forget. She was working at "the big house," and in the afternoon she went to see her aunt. She had brought the sick old lady some new shoes and some chicken broth, but "Miss Amelia" was too weak to even look at the shoes. Pouring the hot liquid into a bowl, Daisy cajoled her into sipping a few spoonfuls of it, then straightened her covers and sat gently clasping her aunt's gnarled hand.

She leaned back in the rocker and began softly singing hymns until the old woman's eyelids closed, and when she left "Miss Amerlia" was resting peacefully. Walking across the field on the warm, plowed soil between the rows of plants, she looked back toward her aunt's house.

Why did she turn around? She would never know. There, only about fifty feet behind her, was the fiercest looking animal she had ever seen. It appeared to be an enormous calf, coat black as coal, fiery eyes glaring at her and as she stared the calf began whirling around and around, growing larger each second. A cloud of dust rose in the air, and suddenly, in a wild burst of fury, it came hurtling after her.

Daisy began to run. Her long legs ran faster than they had ever run before, and the hooves pounding the ground behind her filled her with terror. Her chest began to hurt with every breath. Gathering courage to look back, she saw to her amazement that there was no calf in sight. The field behind her was empty. But she still had only one thought in mind—run! She ran until, weak with exhaustion, she reached her house. While she was recovering, a knock came at the door, and there stood her aunt's best friend.

"Daisy, honey, I'm bringing bad news. Your auntie's passed on. She won't need those new shoes."

"Ohhh … Maggie!" Daisy wailed.

"I saw you walking from her house toward the road, and I hollered at you but all of a sudden you took off running.

"I got me a mirror and put it up to her lips, but there was no breath in her. She must have gone 'bout the time you were lighting out across that field."

"Did you see the big calf coming after me?" asked Daisy.

"Calf? What you talking about?"

The other woman looked incredulous.

Suddenly Daisy understood with frightening clarity.

"Oh, my precious Lord!" she gasped. "That was no real calf; that was a plat-eye!"

Warren and the Werewolf

THE TALL BOY SAT IN THE FRONT ROW, listening so intently to my stories that it was impossible not to notice him. And this was despite formidable distractions, for I was speaking in one of those schools built during the Great Depression, and the wooden auditorium seats creaked with such abominable frequency that I wondered how long I could stand it.

After my performance, the high school student I had noticed joined the group waiting to ask questions. Several times his eye caught mine. I thought he would step forward with some query. He did not. There were two more programs to give, and the day ahead passed more slowly than usual. One by one boys and girls who had a story of their own to relate came up, along with students asking eager questions about how to become a writer. Finally they were gone.

The school was in a small community near Eden, North Carolina, surrounded by peaceful, rural country, and the response to my stories had been exciting. Suddenly the lad in the front row rose from his seat and sauntered toward me. He was wearing a sweat shirt, jeans and sneakers, almost a uniform these days. In the process of gathering up my books from the stage I paused.

"My name is Warren Miller," he began, then, flushed and frowning, he ran his fingers nervously through brownish-blond hair.

"Yes, Warren?" I said.

"I have a story I wondered if you would be interested in, but maybe you don't have enough time."

The cast of a school play was beginning to set up for a practice on the stage behind us.

"If it won't take long," I said.

"I don't think I can tell it with all these kids coming in. May I see you before you leave this afternoon?"

"I won't have but a few minutes then," I said, knowing I would want to start on my drive home. "What is your story about, Warren?"

He hesitated. "Mrs. Roberts. Do you believe in werewolves?" A sudden spark ignited in his eyes.

"I'm not sure, Warren," I answered, taken aback.

By now, students were shouting directions and scenery flats clattered horrendously on stage behind us. He was right. This was no time to talk, and I usually tried to get away as soon as possible after my last program. When I explained this his eyes flashed me a look of appeal.

I weakened. "Well, perhaps a few minutes, Warren, but I can't promise more." Obviously disappointed, he turned away. Did this tall, lanky, not uncomely boy actually have a werewolf story he wanted to tell me? How primitive! Surely not in North Carolina in the 1980s.

During my break before the next program, I leafed mechanically through a magazine, not really seeing the pages. Articles I had read on lycanthropy were beginning to surface in my mind.

I thought of the case of a farmer so obsessed by the belief that he was turning into a wolf that he could no longer plow nor feed his livestock. He left home, living outdoors, where his hair grew into matted tangles that he thought of as fur. At night he emitted weird cries and howls.

And then I recalled a paragraph on werewolves from St. Augustine's *Laws of the Church* that I had once thought interesting enough to commit to memory.

> It is generally believed that by certain witches' spells and the power of the Devil men may be changed into wolves ... but they do not lose their human reason and understanding nor are their minds made the intelligence of a mere beast.
>
> Now this must be understood in this way; namely, that the Devil creates no new nature, but that he is able to make something appear to be which in reality is not. For through no spell nor evil power can the mind, nay not even the body ... be changed into the material limbs and features of any animal ... but a man, is fantastically and by illusion, metamorphosed into an animal, and to himself seems to be a quadruped.

The words "to himself seems to be a quadruped" was to me the key. But what a horrible illusion! And if only he "thinks himself a wolf" can anyone else see him as such?

I closed my unread magazine and accompanied the librarian to the school cafeteria. On the way we passed the werewolf boy in the hall. *Not* "werewolf boy," I thought, angrily. This boy has a name and it is

Warren. I could have sworn he had seen me, but his sharp-featured young face was expressionless. He probably would not come up after the program. I usually can tell the difference between attention seekers and people who have had authentic experiences. I felt a sense of relief as I concluded that he was probably one of the former, and I put the incident out of my mind.

By the time I returned to the auditorium, middle-school students were already filing noisily in for the second program. While I was speaking I heard the door quietly open. There stood Warren. He went over and spoke to the librarian, and she nodded permission for him to sit down. This would be his second session of the day. I wondered how he had wangled permission to miss another class. The questions afterward are usually pretty predictable, but that day someone asked a question I seldom receive.

"Is there such a thing as a ghost or phantom animal?"

What a coincidence to receive this query today. I thought of stories of ghost dogs and ghost horses and replied, "Yes. They are not uncommon."

I devoutly hoped that Warren would not raise his hand at this point and broach the subject of werewolves. That question could open up too many other issues in life—how violence and even the demonic appear to be part of certain criminal personalities, the physical imprint of evil that sometime takes place upon an individual such as Dr. Jekyll who transformed into the evil Mr. Hyde, or a Dorian Gray. To my relief the young man said nothing. It was time to close, for I had already run fifteen minutes over, and the school buses would leave soon.

While students lingered to ask questions, I noticed Warren leaning against the wall beside a window, leafing through a textbook. I suspected he was feigning interest, waiting for others to leave. The students standing in line for autographs were down to five, and as I signed the last book, he put the text under his arm and nonchalantly strolled over to me.

"Mrs. Roberts, do you remember what I was talking with you about this morning?"

"Yes." Of course I remembered, but for some reason the subject filled me with uneasiness.

"I've seen one."

This really startled me, but I said coolly, "Fascinating. You've seen a werewolf?"

"Yes, I have."

In addition to cheek, the boy must have emotional problems. What could I say to help him?

"I'm not the only one who has seen it," he added as if trying to convince me. "It wasn't long ago when—"

He was about to continue when I interrupted with a suggestion. "Warren, why don't we sit up on the stage and talk about it?" I said, trying for a soothing, casual tone. I walked up the five stairs while he, with a kind of bound, vaulted over the row of footlights and was beside me.

"What causes it?" he asked, poised on the edge of the chair beside me leaning forward avidly.

I ignored his question. "Now, tell me what you saw."

"It was late in the afternoon, and I was looking around in the kitchen for something to eat. Nobody was home but me. My brother liked to go hunting with his dog, and I knew he would be out until sometime that night. Mum was usually home by then, and I was wondering whether she had stopped at the store.

"I glanced out the kitchen window thinking if she wasn't coming up the road, she might be still on the shortcut that went through the woods. I didn't see her and decided to go meet her. Thinking it would be dark, I took a flashlight. As I walked along the path through the woods it was not long until I passed a man. At first I thought he might be someone I knew, but he was a stranger. Everyone knows everyone around here, and I was curious, so I turned to look at him. He was really staring at me. That gave me a funny feeling like he wanted to speak to me but wouldn't."

"What did he look like?"

"It's hard to describe. One of the things that struck me was that he had unusually bright, yellowish eyes. I continued down the path, but something made me decide to sit down on a tree trunk and wait, thinking he would have to pass me and then I would say something to get an answer. Instead he stopped before he reached me and sat down upon a big rock about fifty feet behind me.

"I thought maybe he wasn't well, and I called, 'Anything I can do for you, sir?' He didn't answer.

"The sun was going down, and it was especially dark around the rock where he sat. I was getting scared. This path through the woods was hardly ever used, and I went on. When I glanced behind me I saw the figure getting up from the rock, but somehow it didn't move like a man does."

"And then?" I prodded gently.

"I went on walking—he followed. Deciding this guy was stalking me, I turned to confront him, and it was a real shocker. He had no clothes on and seemed to be covered with a kind of grayish fur. His body was so much like that of a man—except its head," he shuddered. "The head was like that of a large wolf with bright yellow eyes. He lunged, and I put up my arms to fend him off. But then he landed right on top of me, and it was—oh, Lord—it was awful.

"I turned the beam of my flashlight on his face, but he had his head down to one side, so that I couldn't see it well. I wanted to run but at first it was like one of those nightmares, Mrs. Roberts. I just couldn't seem to move. Then I dropped the flashlight, pushed him away as hard as I could, and I took off running."

"Were you hurt, Warren?"

"His teeth tore my arm a little. Nothing more.

"In a few minutes, Mom came home, and I tried to tell her about it, but when I said I'd met something half human, half animal, she laughed. Said I was too imaginative. But that week I began to hear stories of people in the village seeing something strange lurking around their houses, staring in their windows when it was near dark. Some were hearing howls. I'm sure it was the same thing I'd seen."

Before I could comment, we heard the footsteps of one of the teachers coming down the auditorium aisle. "Warren, why weren't you outside with the others?" she said in a sharp voice. "You've missed your bus!"

"Oh! I'm sorry."

"Sorry doesn't cut it with me. You're irresponsible! Can you call home and get your mother to come for you?"

"Yes—I mean no. She's working four to twelve this week. I'll walk."

"All that way—ridiculous!" She looked out the auditorium window. It was December. The clouds in the sky were a harbinger of snow, and it was growing darker.

"Where is his house?" I asked.

"Actually, the turn to it is on your way back to the interstate, but you needn't do that. I can get the athletic coach to drop him off—No, I forgot, he's out of town at a conference today."

"Don't worry. I'll take him." I was surprised to hear myself say this because I had not been able to warm up to Warren, and I would be glad to see the last of him. But I felt at least partly to blame for his missing the bus. The teacher insisted on drawing a map for me from the school to the turn to his house and from there to the interstate. She thrust it into my hand.

The train of our conversation in the auditorium had been interrupted, and we drove for a while in silence. Warren sat rigid staring straight ahead. I could see the tense set of his jaw. It quivered slightly. Perhaps he was close to tears because the teacher had embarrassed him before a visitor to the school. How mortified he must be. The road that turned off this one and led to Warren's home was perhaps three miles away. I would be happy when we reached it.

"So you didn't see this creature again yourself?"

"No, not until yesterday when it was almost dark. What attracted my attention was some weird growls outside. When I looked out the bushes were moving just beneath the kitchen window."

"And?"

"And then staring through the window at me was the thing I had met in the woods. Its eyes were blazing like they had before and the teeth were pointed."

Warren's expression twisted in such a grimace of fear and revulsion at the memory that he put up his hands and covered his face. For the first time I noticed the long reddish scar on the side of his right hand and arm. Despite my skepticism I could feel the hair on the nape of my neck rise. I tried to talk normally.

"Were you at home alone, Warren?"

"Yes." He turned away, and we both fell silent. But I was aware that he was nervous, even trembling slightly. I searched for something to say that sounded sympathetic.

"I'm sorry. That must have been a frightening experience. Are there any wild dogs in the area?"

He shook his head. We were silent for a long time after that. Finally Warren spoke, his jaw quivering so slightly it was almost imperceptible.

"Mrs. Roberts."

"Yes."

"Do you think if a werewolf bites you that you become a werewolf, too?"

"Warren, there is really no more I can tell you about werewolves. I don't even believe they exist. Why don't you consider doing a paper on their history in folklore?"

"Oh, yes they do!" His voice seemed to break with the strength of his emotion. "They exist, Mrs. Roberts!"

I glanced at him in shocked surprise and noticed that he was salivating.

"Warren!"

His teeth were clicking together, making ever so faint a sound.

"I think that if the teeth just scratch your flesh, it can make you a werewolf," he said, bending toward me with a quick, sharp intake of breath.

I was so frightened by now that it was difficult not to show it. I made no reply. A light snow was beginning to fall. The county road sign where the map indicated I was to stop and let him out must be just ahead, or we had passed it. No, thank heaven, there it was. We pulled to a stop, and his hand with the ugly red scar reached for mine. I jerked away, and when I did his upper lip curled slightly so that I saw his teeth.

"Warren. This is where you get out."

His amber eyes glittered. "Turn here and take me all the way home," he ordered. At that moment a patrol car going in the other direction stopped, and Warren shrank back. The officer rolled down his window.

"Lady, are you lost? This is a lonely stretch of road, and I wouldn't want anything to happen to you."

"Tell him no!" barked Warren, followed by a more cautious low, hoarse whisper. "I know what I'm doing."

His hand reached for the wheel, trying to turn it, but I held it fast and prayed the officer would not drive on.

"I've got a map here the school drew for me, but I'm confused, officer," I said plaintively. "Would you look at it?"

The officer hesitated. I was ready to scream at him—something, anything that would bring him to the window of my Honda. But he seemed to change his mind and got out of the patrol car. As he did Warren leaped from the passenger seat beside me to the ground in one smooth motion and was off down the road with such speed that he almost seemed to float.

The officer's eyes looked after the boy curiously. "What got into him? Sure can run, can't he?"

Then, wafted back on the wind, came a hideous, long drawn-out cry. The officer turned, his eyes scanning the fields.

"Lordy! What kind of critter was that?"

MONSTERS IN THE FLESH

The Jersey Devil

Born in thunder—lightning—rain! Does this creature live again?

THE PEOPLE OF THE PINE BARRENS call it the "Jersey Devil," and some do not take it lightly. Although both Estillville and Burlington claim him, the real site of this creature's birth is said to be Leeds Point—a lonely, marshy promontory between the Pinelands and the ocean. Most of the reported exploits of the Jersey Devil have occurred in this vast, desolate area of the state covered with scrub pine, cedar, and swamp which extends from the Delaware River east to the shores of the Atlantic.

Over the years, there have been attempts to civilize this region, but they have never really succeeded; its heart is still dark and full of mystery.

Here you may stumble upon the ruins of some long abandoned village. Deer may cross your path or an occasional bear, but you are unlikely to see another human face.

Our story began on a wild and stormy night in 1737. The setting: a backwoods farm at Leeds Point, in South Jersey. Lightning flashed, thunder reverberated, and a torrent of rain swept the woods and pelted the roof of the cabin like hailstones. Upstairs in tiny rooms slept a dozen children, and below, in the weird, dancing shadows of a kerosene lamp, a woman lay in labor. This was Mother Leeds' thirteenth child. Beside her sat two old crones, one holding a cold cloth to the brow of the sufferer. Old Betsy Pettit's hoarse, urgent words rubbed together like dead leaves,

"Bear down, girl. Bear down."

Mother Leeds clutched Betsy's hand in an iron grip, and even above the the wind in the pines outside her angry rebellious shriek could be heard.

"If I must bear this child, *may it become the Devil himself!*"

The two women attending her cringed, eyes wide with terror. Both women knew Mother Leeds was already struggling to take care of twelve children, but no need to tempt providence. There was a brilliant flash of lightning close by, followed by a long roll of crashing thunder, and Betsy Pettit started up from her chair, trembling.

"She shouldn't spout off about the Devil on a night like this," she exclaimed.

"Ay, and when 'tis almost midnight," agreed Meg, her face darkening with disapproval as she stared down at the pain-contorted face on the pillow.

There was a temporary letup in the downpour, and from outside came the eerie *who—who—who* of an owl.

"Did you hear that, Betsy?" asked Meg, the hardier of the two. Her faded blue eyes that usually held a fierce, challenging expression were filled with fright. "An owl's hoot. 'Tis a sure sign of disaster." She nodded her grizzled head sagely.

Betsy Pettit and Meg Barnwell might have been sisters for all appearances—both with blue eyes, stringy gray hair, and parchment-like skin.

A flash of lightning illuminated the room, and wind whistled through the cracks.

"Is the water hot enough? Do ye have the towels ready?"

"Ay."

Thunder that sounded like heavy artillery shook the cabin and on its heels another scream from the woman on the straw pallet rent the air. She tried to strike her head against the log wall of the cabin.

"Hold her! Help me hold her," shouted Meg, grasping Mother Leeds by the arm. "Afore she hurts herself."

"Lord a mercy. I didn't know she was goin' to do that." Betsy clutched at the writhing woman who was trying to throw herself against the wall again.

"I see the baby's head. Hold her, Betsy!"

Within minutes the women delivered a beautiful healthy boy.

"Is there more hot water, Betsy?"

"Yes."

"Then make her a cup of tea and some for we uns, too."

With an arm around her shoulders, Betsy supported Mother Leeds, tipping the hot liquid to her lips. The woman took a deep draught, sighed, and lay back weak and exhausted with the baby. For a moment she gazed down at the little boy in the crook of her arm. Then, with a long, piercing shriek, she fell back on the bed in a faint. Only Betsy's quick hand kept the infant from falling to the floor.

Both women stared in dismay. A terrible transformation was taking place. The healthy baby boy they had just delivered was rapidly changing. His skin was turning darker, his ears were growing larger and more pointed by the second, his nostrils were coarsening and flaring, his jaws were elongating like lightning and widening into a vicious snarl. The shoulder bones began to sweep upward in tall peaks while clawed hands gradually emerged from the tips of the short webbed arms attached to the upper body.

So horrified were the two women they could scarcely bear to look—nor could they tear their eyes away. The creature resembled a small dragon, its short reptilian form tapering into a wildly slashing tail. As they stared, the infant-turned-monster gazed viciously at them for a terrifying moment, reached down, pummeled Mother Leeds, and then lunged out the door.

From that time on there were constant rumors of frightening appearances—first from one place and then another. The people of the barrens near Burlington, New Jersey endured savage raids on flocks and herds. They would start their round of morning chores to find cattle slaughtered and torn apart by some animal-like creature possessed of hideous strength. Several villagers formed a posse to track down Mrs. Leed's devil-son, but could never find him. Every time a weird shape was seen at the height of a Down Jersey thunderstorm or strange footprints were found along the banks of the Mullica River or a moving shadow startled someone in the darkness of the barrens, it was said to be the Leeds Devil—later known as the Jersey Devil.

What is fact and what is fiction? There can be no doubt that the birth—perhaps of a deformed baby born to Mrs. Leeds—was followed by stories that it had escaped and was raiding farmers' poultry and livestock. There was such an uproar that people in Burlington, New Jersey demanded an exorcism to rid them of this plague.

In 1740, with bell, book, and candle, the exorcism took place. There was a large gathering of the frightened faithful, and a clergyman, invoking God's protection from the Jersey Devil, sprinkled holy water on all who filed past. This was designed to frighten the creature away for one hundred years, but evidently exorcisms are more effective in frightening away spirits than monsters, for sightings continued to occur. An early description of the Leeds Devil is attributed to Larner Leeds, thought to have been the creature's father.

> It was neither beast, nor man, nor spirit, but a hellish brew of all three. It was beside a pond when I came upon it. I stopped and did not move. I could not move. It was dashing its tail to and fro in the pond and rubbing its horns against a tree trunk. It was as large as a moose with leather wings. It had cloven hooves as big around as an oak's trunk. After it was through with the tree, it yielded an awful scream as if it were a pained man, and then flew across the pond until I could see it no more.

Larner undoubtedly exaggerated, but perhaps we should allow for his state of mind at the time he witnessed the strange creature.

Over the years the Leeds Devil came to be called the Jersey Devil. It is said that the former King of Spain and brother of Napoleon, Joseph Bonaparte, who lived in Bordentown, New Jersey from 1816 to 1839, saw the Jersey Devil while hunting in the woods. Another story is that Captain Kidd, on his ill-fated trip up the Atlantic coast to Boston, buried treasure along Barnegat Bay and left one of his crew to forever guard it. Legend has it that the pirate became a comrade of the Jersey Devil and the pair walked the shore together at night.

With the coming of 1840 the people of South Jersey were particularly apprehensive, for they were still hearing stories from their elders that this was the year the Jersey Devil would return with a vengeance.

The new year arrived and with it came an uproar over the rash of attacks on chickens and sheep. Terrifying shrieks were heard at night and strange tracks appeared around homes. Posses went out only to return without success. In the years that followed the livestock attacks continued and appearances of the Jersey Devil were reported in Haddonfield and Bridgeton during the winter of 1873 and 1874. In the 1880s they said it carried off "anything that moved" in the Pine Barrens, and during the 1890s sightings cropped up at Smithfield, at Long Beach Island, at Brigantine Beach, its home ground of Leeds Point, and again in Haddonfield.

In 1899 the Devil was said to appear in North Jersey along the New York border, and *The Rockland Independent* reported that sheep were disturbed for a number of nights by the most ungodly screams from the vicinity of Pascack River in Spring Valley, New York. A "winged serpent" was reported at Hyenga Lake that eventually headed back toward Leed's Point, leaving unusual tracks behind it along the way.

By the turn of the century many South Jerseyites were convinced that the Pine Barrens was the home of some eerie creature. *Jersey Genesis* quotes J. Elfreth Watkins as writing this description in 1905 for his syndicated column in the Sunday supplements.

> Accompanied, as it usually is, by the howling of dogs and the hooting of owls, there can be no surer forerunner of disaster. Where the Barrens line the shore it flits from one desolate grass-grown dune to another and is especially watchful upon those wild heights when coasting schooners, driving their prows into the sand, pound to splinters upon the bars and distribute upon the waves their freight of goods and human lives.

The Jersey Devil continued to be regarded as a harbinger of disaster before wars, and sightings were reported in the late 1930s before World War II. They continue to this day. But nothing was to match his frightening multiple appearances during the third week of January in 1909. Emerging from his accustomed haunts in the Pine Barrens, he strolled through the Delaware Valley, fascinating some and affrighting others. From January 16-23 thousands saw either the creature or the monstrous footprints he left behind him.

Among the more interesting of many comparisons were those of a kangaroo-horse and prehistoric lizard, but people soon realized that all these nomenclatures described just one creature—the Jersey Devil. Fear swept through south Jersey towns. During that week schools and factories closed as posses fanned out over the mud flats and farm land between the Delaware River and the sea, but with no success.

Within a twelve-hour period the creature was sighted by residents of Bristol, Pennsylvania, and Woodbury, New Jersey.

"I heard a hissing and something white flew across the street," said Thack Cozzens of Woodbury. "I saw two spots of phosphorous—the eyes of the beast. There was a white cloud, like escaping steam from an engine. It moved as fast as an auto." Cozzens saw it on Saturday night, January 16 shortly after he had left the Woodbury Hotel.

That same night in Bristol, Pennsylvania, three people in different parts of town were to know a different fear from any they had ever experienced. John McOwen had gone to bed and was sleeping peacefully when he was awakened at two o'clock in the morning by the sound of his baby daughter crying. He was in her bedroom holding the baby, trying to calm her, when he heard odd whistling noises outside.

"I looked out the window and was amazed to see something

hopping along the tow path beside the Delaware Canal," said McOwen, describing it as similar to a large eagle.

Meanwhile over on Buckley Street Officer James Sackville was trudging along through the snow making his rounds when he became aware of the neighborhood dogs barking and howling. "I never heard such a row!" It made him feel uneasy. Then, like many experienced police officers, he felt rather than heard the presence of something behind him. Whirling, he saw a dark moving shape, and ran toward it. As he drew closer, he saw that the creature was winged and had the face of some queer looking animal, but it hopped like a bird. The screams it emitted were horrible indeed. Sackville pointed his revolver at it and began firing. His target took off, flying low as if to gain lift for the enormous body, then soared out of view.

Postmaster E.W. Minster, also of Bristol, New Jersey, woke up with a headache at about the time McOwen was pacing the floor trying to quiet his baby. He heard something between a squawk and a whistle outside and looked out his window toward the river to see a creature in flight, long thick neck thrust forward with thin attenuated wings and short legs. Somewhat reptilian, the front legs were shorter than the rear. There were tracks in the yards of some Bristol residents the following morning.

The next stop for the Jersey Devil was Burlington, and various traces of its presence were reported on Sunday by residents in and around the town. The contents of garbage cans had been raided and partially devoured. Townspeople found footprints that seemed to lead into yards and vanish, skip from one rooftop to another, and climb trees. Many stayed inside that Monday behind locked doors and windows. There was real panic, and as reports of tracks in the rural communities came in farmers set out steel traps and organized search parties with dogs to hunt down the Jersey Devil.

The dogs sniffed the tracks but refused to follow them, so the searchers went on. They would observe tracks on the ground for several miles, only to have the tracks suddenly stop in the Pinelands. If it appears that the many posses sent out to search should have found the creature, we must remember that this area covers over a million acres of swamp and woods—one-fourth of the entire state.

There was scarcely a South Jersey town where sightings of the Jersey Devil were not reported during the third week of January in 1909. A report from Glassboro described the creature as having three toes with claws. (These resemble tracks found in South Carolina eighty years later in 1989!)

The book titled *The Jersey Devil* by James F. McCloy and Ralph Miller Jr. describes places and details of sightings over the years, some in the 1930s and others in the 1950s and '60s. It includes one of the more savage instances near the Mullica River in April of 1966 when Steven Silkotch went out to do his farm chores one morning and found the carcasses of thirty-one ducks, three geese and two German shepherds. The heavy collar of one of his dogs had been chewed to pieces and its ninety-pound body dragged a quarter of a mile. Tracks led into the same woods along the Mullica River where they have been found before.

David Wilcox, branch manager of the Atlantic County Library West, travels from his home to work at Hammonton every day. The drive takes twenty-five minutes. He travels about fifteen minutes of it through the Barrens, and of course, he has heard for years that they are the home of the Jersey Devil. Wilcox describes his drive.

"In the fall I leave the library in Hammonton at dusk, and the forest is dark as I enter it. No afterglow from the sunset, no street lamp along the way—just pitch-black. You can't see a thing! The only way I know where I am is when my headlights illuminate a named crossroads sign. I know some people—quite unimaginative in most respects—who simply won't drive through there at night," says Wilcox.

"A region aboriginal in savagery," a writer wrote for the *Atlantic* magazine in 1859, and it is not so different today. Since the Barrens have successfully resisted civilization, is it possible that some primeval being rises from the amber-black waters of this ancient wilderness? Does it occasionally emerge dark and wet to stalk the roads, to blunder bewildered and fiercely angry into the path of men?

Born in thunder—lightning—rain! Does this creature live again?

That question remains unanswered.

Ogopogo the Sea Monster

As we sit on the beach beside a magnificent lake in British Columbia, we hear the sudden sound of waves lapping turbulently at the shore. We look up expecting to see a sizable boat. Instead we see a creature with a head the size of a horse followed by large snake-like coils glistening in the sunlight. Undulating rapidly, it hurtles past us. Has the filming of a movie disturbed our peaceful day, or have we been transported back in time—say a million years?

There have always been tales of terrifying dragons and sea monsters handed down from one generation to the next. "Just legends," they told us as children; "long extinct," they taught us in college. Believing them, we may be surprised to discover that stories of sea serpents abound, not just in folklore but in the accounts of early American sea captains.

Gloucester, Massachusetts has this fascinating affidavit about a sea serpent written by a ship's captain, Solomon Allen, in 1817 and signed before a justice of the peace.

> I, Solomon Allen III, of Gloucester, in the County of Essex, Shipmaster, dispose and say: that I have seen a strange marine animal that I believe to be a sea serpent, in the harbor in Gloucester.
>
> I should judge him to be in length between 80 and 90 feet and about the size of a half barrel, apparently having joints from his head to his tail .... His head was formed something like the head of a rattlesnake but nearly as large as the head of a horse .... When he disappeared he sunk apparently directly down and would appear at 200 yards from where he disappeared, in two minutes. His color was dark brown and I did not see spots upon him.

A similar affidavit was signed by a Matthew Gaffney who was in a dinghy that came within 30 feet of this "strange marine serpent."

The "serpent" evidently lived for several months in a fairly small section of the ocean and was seen by hundreds of people. The natives of Gloucester spent a lot of time on the sea, often voyaging far from home, and they were familiar with all types of marine life—porpoises, whales, sharks, squid, rays, and many other sea creatures. But they had never seen anything of such length and with humps on its back that appeared and disappeared as it moved.

In the past century, one theory after another by means of which unimaginative naysayers limited both achievement and knowledge has been discredited. Exceeding the speed of sound, putting men on the moon, and performing surgery without a scalpel are among the many feats once thought foolhardy and currently taken for granted.

It now seems that the presence of large unidentified swimming objects is meeting this same derision and lack of serious scientific interest. We research the intelligence of dolphins, worry about preserving the nests of bald eagles, divert roads to avoid damaging obscure varieties of sunflowers, but seem unable to arouse any sustained scientific investigation into sightings of sea serpents! How like us! Only when sensitive photographic equipment became accessible to interested amateur investigators did graphic evidence begin to proliferate.

Our story begins with the Indians of the Okanagan Valley in British Columbia who feared a mysterious creature inhabiting Okanagan Lake they called Naitaka. Believing the immense and always hungry Naitaka must be placated with sacrifices, they often took some small animal to toss to the monster on voyages across the lake. Although early white settlers had startling experiences with something in the lake, they were more reluctant to report it than the Indians.

Meanwhile, as the population of the valley continued to grow, sightings of the being, renamed Ogopogo, became more frequent.

"I call it simply a USO—an unidentified swimming object—rather than any monster," says former schoolteacher Ms. Gaal in her common sense way. Now a columnist for the *Kelowna Daily Courier*, she has written a book entitled *Ogopogo*, detailing innumerable USO sightings of the early Canadian pioneers as well as those of modern natives and visitors.

Early British Columbia settler and guide John McDougall, part Indian himself, knew the native customs well. McDougall usually carried a sacrifice with him when he went out on the lake, in keeping with Indian custom, but one day, remembering that he had promised to help his friend John Allison at Westbank with his haying, McDougall forgot. Tethering his two horses behind a large canoe, he set out across the lake without the sacrifice.

Suddenly the two horses swimming leisurely along behind his canoe appeared to be in trouble. He brought the canoe to a standstill and, turning, he saw the neighing animals begin to tread water. It appeared that they were being drawn under by some extraordinary force from below. Before his canoe suffered the same fate, he pulled his sheath knife and cut the rope to the horses. Then, fearing for his own life, McDougall paddled away at top speed. No sign of the two horses was ever found.

Mrs. Ruth Richardson, now living in Cashmere, Washington, will always remember an experience that occurred when she was a child of ten playing on the beach at Okanagan Landing, a short distance from her home. Here is her account.

"I was thoroughly absorbed in building a sand castle when I began to hear the swishing sound of waves. My first thought was that waves were coming in and would wash my castle away. I looked toward the lake. There was a strange creature out there just offshore that was very still and seemed to be looking over at me as if I were some kind of curiosity. About three feet of him was out of the water. We simply stared at each other for awhile and then he seemed to be backing up and going down under the water, so I went on playing.

"All at once the swishing sound was very loud and close, and when I turned, I saw that it was the same creature and he was much too close. I was terribly frightened although he did nothing but just sit very still and gaze at me, so I ran for the house."

A grown woman now, Mrs. Richardson believes that the creature she saw had scales "that looked like shale rock" and three points or fins on its back.

Arlene Gaal's interest in the sightings began when she moved to Kelowna, British Columbia, in 1968. Lake Okanagan was only about a fifteen-minute drive from her home, and she heard about the sea monster everyone called Ogopogo. Those who had seen the strange creature believed in its existence in the lake; those who had not seen it were skeptics.

At the time Ms. Gaal began her investigation into the phenomena of the water monster she had never seen it, but by collecting accounts of sightings from reputable people, she became the acknowledged authority on Ogopogo, documenting scores of dramatic sightings. In some areas the water of the lake is as much as a thousand feet deep, and there is also a volcanic cone on the lake floor with depths probably considerably greater than the lake floor itself.

One warm afternoon when Aileen Gaal was taking a walk near the lake she had her own experience. The surface was mirror calm with not a boat to be seen. Suddenly she became aware that there were two shadows traveling beneath the surface of the water. This is usually the result of clouds passing overhead, but today the sky was clear, and as she stared down again, bewildered, she realized that the dark shape was in two parts and moving purposefully toward the south side of the bridge. Then she saw massive, rolling waves like those created by a submarine surfacing, and an enormous dark object broke water.

"Oh my God! No!" she cried out.

Realizing her camera was in the car, she dashed back after it. When she returned the surface of the lake, hitherto calm, had waves upon it resembling those left by a boat's wake. The creature was still right where she had left it, lying languidly on the surface of the lake. She shot pictures until it submerged in water about three hundred feet deep. Her photos while it was above water show an animal forty to fifty feet long.

After her personal experience Ms. Gaal began to collect accounts of sightings with even greater enthusiasm. Of equal interest are her descriptions of expeditions to film Ogopogo spurred by the interest of TV producers in England, the United States, Japan, and other countries. But the most fascinating incidents still continue to be the sightings.

The following are excerpted from literally scores of incidents in her book, *Ogopogo*.

"When passengers on a Greyhound bus all see the creature as they did on June 29, 1950, it makes it hard for the skeptics to dispute it," she says.

Driver Gordon Radcliffe was headed south from Kelowna to Summerland when he saw something out on the lake about three hundred yards offshore. He immediately pulled off the road, and he and his fifteen passengers piled out hurriedly to look.

"We all stood there unable to believe our eyes," said Radcliffe. "The head was large. The body long with a dull sheen. We watched it for about five minutes as it submerged and reappeared above the water several times." His story was substantiated by all the Greyhound passengers.

Boat squadron leader Bruce Miller and his wife were driving along

Naramata Road above the lake one summer Sunday evening when they saw something in the lake and pulled off on the shoulder. Down below them they had a ringside view of a long object that glided along through the water with an undulating motion, coiled its back, then relaxed the coils and lay quietly for a while as if resting, sometimes raising its head majestically to survey the lake. At intervals its tail would rise, and there would be a sharp splash as it submerged. The Millers described the creature as about seventy-five feet long, lithe and sinewy.

On another occasion a crowd of people sunning on Penticton beach in the summer of 1951 stood and watched as the USO glided along the calm surface of the lake, keeping its head under and traveling in a straight line parallel to the shore line. All of its legendary humps were visible.

That same summer seven Red Cross workers in the blood transfusion service were driving along north of Penticton when Mrs. J. Thorkelson looked out and saw something unusual swimming in the lake. She shouted to the driver, June McArthur, to stop, and all seven women jumped out, watching in astonishment while a brownish-green creature about twenty-five feet long sailed smoothly past. Riding high in the water, the animal had three large humps trailing behind it and was going in the direction of Kelowna.

In 1977 the Lake Monster debuted early, before the hot weather it usually favors, and one of the best sightings took place at Sarsons Beach in Kelowna. Lillian Vogelgesang and her nine-year-old daughter, Jamie, were out on the beach, Ms. Vogelgesang picking up pebbles and her daughter racing ahead of her in the direction of the dock. Suddenly Jamie gave a frightened scream and her mother ran toward her. In the water at the end of the dock the child was gazing at a creature the length of a house that was surfacing at least three feet out of the water.

"Mommy, it has feet," yelled Jamie and ran to the safety of her mother's arms. Ms. Vogelgesang saw five visible humps on its back. As they stood watching the water foam and froth around the sea creature they were joined by Mrs. Brome, a neighbor who had run up when she heard the child's frantic screams. The three stood and watched as the Lake Monster took off at a fantastic speed, leaving a V-shaped wake behind it.

In August of 1979, three generations of the Reiger family, Adam, his son Jim, and his grandson Orry, were spending an afternoon at Okanagan Center fishing from a boat on the lake. It was a hot day and the lake surface was calm. Suddenly the water was in a state of foaming turmoil and the churning was heading toward them with something rising from its midst. The Kokanee craft which had been clearly visible made a hasty retreat. The Reigers soon saw why. To their shock, they found themselves being paced by a massive, dinosaur-like creature that Adam estimated to be about twenty tons.

They were so fascinated by the sight of the creature that they gazed at it, oblivious to danger. They saw four legs—two in front and two in back—those in front, jointed at the elbow, were moving forward in a breaststroke while the back legs pushed. Its tail was extremely long. The back was about three feet above the water and the neck, emerging from a heavy shoulder structure, moved in a manner indicating that the creature was feeding beneath the surface. When it had evidently satiated its hunger, it submerged like a submarine into the depths of the lake.

Of course there are those who arrive at Kelowna full of eagerness to see the creature and sit safely on shore, some mumbling incantations to themselves such as: "Ogopogo, come we pray—show yourself to us today!" But the serpent is not known to be so obliging, and even a ferry boat captain who traversed the lake daily never saw Ogopogo until after his retirement.

Continued sightings over the years, however, are now attracting the attention of marine scientists and media alike. With lake monsters in common, it was inevitable that there would be comparisons between "Nessie" in Scotland and "Ogopogo" in British Columbia. Photos of Nessie, better known as the Loch Ness monster, included in Ms. Gaal's book greatly resemble photos, sketches, and descriptions of the now famous Okanagan Lake Monster, Ogopogo. But the Folden Film is probably the most talked-about proof of the unidentified marine creature harbored by the waters of Okanagan Lake. Ms. Gaal describes her viewing of the eight-millimeter film shot by Art Folden of British Columbia, which she was invited to judge for its authenticity.

"As the reel rolled, a dark shadow appeared near the surface. Then quite suddenly the shadow became a dark hump which disappeared" below the water.

"The next portion intrigued me greatly as a long, sinuous, snake-like serpent at least seventy feet in length or longer glided ever so smoothly just below the surface ... at a rapid speed. At the front a serpent-like head, which naturally was shadowy as no features could be made out below the surface, tapered into a slightly thicker body section. The body, by no means elephantine in shape as is the plesiosaur, narrowed into a tail-like structure thinner than the rest of the unidentified swimming objects [in the lake] but not that much.

"Suddenly the object disappeared, only to reappear as a distinct black object moving at such a rapid speed that the quiet waters churned up much more foamy spray than the average motorboat would ever create. As fast as it surfaced, it submerged once more and resurfaced, again churning up the waters to create a milky froth. I knew at once that what I was witnessing were the undulating movements so often described as the object took off across the lake at a tremendous speed.

"It completely submerged—straight down—but as it was lowering itself into the depths, the long sinuous snake-like body was visible for a few seconds before it disappeared."

Ms. Gaal reviewed the film twice and was convinced she had seen an authentic record of a form of life in Okanagan Lake that has "changed many skeptics into believing what was once considered to be only folklore."

Besides actual sightings by large groups of people, she considers the Folden Film of 1968, the Thal Film of 1980 and the Boisselle Video of 1982 as the best proofs (up to the date of her book) of the existence of Ogopogo. Study of the footage by experts should help produce the details scientists need.

Writer R.P. MacLean brings out how remarkably alike areas are that have these sightings. Loch Ness and Okanagan lie in almost the same latitude. Both are long and narrow, having areas of great depth. Both were formed by cataclysmic shifts of the earth's crust. They have similar water temperatures and contain almost identical varieties of fish. Of course, the sightings are unlikely to be of one creature. It must be a species in both places. In Okanagan Lake there have sometimes been sightings of two or more creatures of different sizes frolicking together. When conflicting reports come in, it is likely the sea creatures were seen in various stages of development.

Hundreds of people have gone on record with affidavits over the past twenty years as having seen the creature.

"They are reputable individuals and groups of people who have absolutely nothing to gain by lying," says fifty-year-old Ms. Gaal, who is herself a graduate of the University of Victoria; among witnesses are "a priest, an Air Force major, a surgeon and a police officer."

Witnesses describe seeing a snake-like body darkish-green or brown varying from twenty to seventy feet in length and with two or more visible humps an equal distance apart. As it undulates swiftly through the water, sometimes a head is seen at a distance resembling that of a horse, but at closer range it is more that of a reptile or serpent. Viewers report watching the creature thrash about in one spot or glide slowly over the calm waters of the lake, alternately surfacing and submerging like a submarine with massive waves flowing off the top.

Ogopogo, as we shall have to continue calling it for lack of a more scientific name, has never attempted to harm anyone, although if attacked it would probably try to defend itself. It has certainly been wise enough to swim off at high speed and even submerge when boats have tried to pursue it. Hopefully, if these rare creatures are discovered, Canadian endangered species legislation will protect them from harm.

Dr. Edward F. Menhinick, a zoologist at the University of North Carolina at Charlotte, said, "Every form of plant and animal life is an important clue to the history of life on Earth. We must take care to preserve and not destroy keys to the past for they may open the door to a better future for all of us."

He emphasizes that efforts to find out more about Ogopogo should not be abandoned but should proceed with the utmost care using advanced methods for underwater investigating.

The problem most people have in accepting Ogopogo is that it appears to be a sea serpent and conventional wisdom holds that "'sea serpents' just can't exist along with nuclear submarines and space walks." Yet in 1938 a lungfish known as a latimeria—considered to have been extinct for eons—was dredged up on the South African coast. And when fishermen in the Indian Ocean hauled up a coelecanth, scientists couldn't believe their eyes because textbooks said it had been extinct for tens of millions of years. Likewise, in 1976 a U.S. Navy ship captured a five-meter-long creature with two thousand teeth—never before seen.

A National Geographic Report estimates that each year scientists discover and classify 15 new reptiles or amphibians, 50 new mammals, 100 new fish, 15 new birds and at least 5,000 new insects. Obviously all the species of creatures on this planet have not yet been discovered.

In 1977 a Japanese trawler off the New Zealand coast netted a 30-foot, two-ton sea reptile resembling those of 130 million years ago. Professor Fujio Byasude of Tokyo Fisheries University who studied photographs of the creature said it looked like a prehistoric plesiosaurus. Fishing company executive Michihiko Yano told reporters it was kept on board for only a short time as the crew feared the decomposition that had set in would contaminate their catch. Japanese newspapers called the creature the South Pacific Nessie.

Of course, Nessie, in the Great Glenn of the Scottish Highlands, is the best known, although it is now believed that they are seeing not one creature but a family of many, for the loch is as deep as 900 feet. The two prominent North American mystery sea creatures are Champie at Lake Champlain and, of course, the internationally famous Ogopogo at Okanagan Lake. It seems amazing that by now there could be any question left.

If we cannot accept the existence of this unusual creature in the waters of Okanagan, is it really logical to believe that perfect strangers to the area, ignorant of the phenomena, see this lake and hallucinate sea serpents?

"Come in August," Arlene Gaal says. "There are more sightings then than in any other month. When I get up and the weather is warm and sunny, I tell myself, there will be sightings reported. This is an Ogopogo kind of day!"

The Lizard Man

IN THE SUMMER OF 1988 in the warm, humid South Carolina Low Country, the curtains opened on an extraordinary drama. The place was a small town called Bishopville. The characters were carloads of tourists who anticipated seeing an extraordinary spectacle.

But why not let Liston Truesdale, the former sheriff of Lee County, South Carolina, give us his side of the story. Though Truesdale has a soft drawl and folksy manner, he doesn't fit the northern stereotype of a redneck southern sheriff. First of all, he is extremely intelligent. A graduate of the University of South Carolina, he has also completed training at the National FBI Academy at Quantico, Virginia. His law enforcement career began as a city police officer in 1955, and before his recent retirement, he served as sheriff for nineteen years. He also received his home state's prestigious Palmetto Award for public service.

Truesdale leaned back in his beige leather chair, a chest of newspaper clippings at his feet and began, "Now on with the true story of the lizard man behind the media hype." The first bizarre event happened in 1988, about the middle of the summer.

"On July 14, Chris Davis, a quiet, shy young man, left work at McDonald's in Camden at ten o'clock to drive home. Home was Bishopville, twenty-five miles distant. As Chris drove he munched on a hamburger, the supper he had not had time for earlier. The two-lane blacktop led through the Brown Town section and Scape Ore Swamp, and it was during the stretch through the swamp that he felt a series of hard jolts on the right side of the car. "Right rear tire," thought Davis, and braking, he pulled off on the shoulder. "A flat." Turning up the rock music station so he could hear it better outside, he began changing the tire.

"He was just replacing the tools in the trunk when there was the sharp crack of branches snapping behind him in the brush at the edge of the swamp. Turning, he was appalled to see an immense creature about ten feet tall coming toward him. Chris dashed from behind the car and leaped into the driver's seat, but before he could turn on the ignition he felt the impact of a heavy blow strike the back of his Toyota Celica. Despite the fact that the emergency brake was on, the car hurtled forward several feet, and while his trembling fingers were turning the key in the ignition, the creature began trying to open the door.

"Flooring the gas pedal, Chris Davis took off, but not quite fast enough, for the dark shape of what appeared to be a paw or a hand hanging down reached across the window. Whatever it was had leaped on top of his car and was holding on. Swerving, hoping the velocity would throw it off, Davis drove like a maniac as he approached Bishopville, but he could not be sure whether his unwanted rider was still clinging to the Celica's roof or not. Blowing the horn as he skidded into the yard, Chris jumped from the car, leaving the headlights on, and raced for the front door.

"When his father, Tom Davis, heard the horn blowing he ran to the door to meet Chris, taking the steps two at a time.

"There's something out there!" Chris shouted.

"Davis, an engineer who heads the electronics department at the local Campbell Soup plant, hurried out to check. He didn't see anyone nor see anything unusual, but Chris was so badly shaken his parents spent the next two hours trying to calm him down. They didn't report their son's experience until later, when this became the first documented appearance of the creature."

Coincidentally, that same day the sheriff's office at Bishopville, South Carolina, was called about an incident almost as bizarre.

"This couple reported that their car had been mysteriously damaged," said Truesdale.

"When my deputy and I responded to the call of Tom and Mary Wayes who lived near Bishopville, we found the car beside the house with scratches and dirt all over the vehicle. Its top was covered with what appeared to be dog tracks. Some of the chrome parts were ripped loose and chewed—the teeth marks visible on the metal. A piece of chrome was torn partly off the side of the car, and both men tried to see how much strength it would take to pull it further. They couldn't do it.

"Another exterior piece of heavy chrome was simply broken off," said Truesdale, staring down at pictures showing the damage. "Beneath the hood, part of the armature had been severed, not with a saw but as if someone had reached in, jerked at it and just snapped it off with their hand. The car was mangled in a peculiar way. It didn't resemble any vandalism we had ever seen."

In the living room of his spacious beige brick home, the former sheriff paused for a sip of Coke, thinking about the near chaos in his office.

"Soon we were getting reports from all over the place of a strange creature being seen in the vicinity of the swamp. But nothing had been reported yet from the Davis boy," he recalled.

"Now Scape Ore Swamp is large. It's what we call a black water swamp with a creek running through the middle and about three-quarters of a mile of swamp on either side. The place has alligators, and the biggest bobcat I've ever seen was shot in it. No telling what else is in that swamp. The trees are mostly black gums with a sprinkling of maples, sweet gums, poplars, cottonwoods and oaks. Those woods are so thick a hunter won't even take a coon dog in there.

"Some of the people in Brown Town were beginning to talk about the 'Lizard Man' saying that he was green. It all sounded pretty silly to me, and I wanted to get to the bottom of the thing as soon as possible and solve it.

"I sent out a call for people who had experienced anything strange to come in and make a statement. One of the first was Tom Davis who brought in his son, Chris, and the boy told me about his experience of two weeks before. I don't think he wanted to come in. He's a shy sort and I gathered that he was even more reluctant to tell the story because he was speeding, probably illegally, to shake the thing off his car. He said his impression was that the creature was hairy rather than having a skin like a lizard. That sounds like stories I've read about yeti.

"Anyway, another fellow named George Holloman Jr. came in, and we took his statement. It seems he was riding his bicycle at night and decided to stop at an outdoor artesian well on the edge of town to get a drink of water. He said he sat down and leaned back to smoke a cigarette and relax when his attention was attracted by what he thought was a dead tree across the road. He later told this to the newspapers, too.

"He said what he thought was a tree moved. A car passed and as the lights swept the side of the road large, fiery eyes shone in the darkness in the direction he had been looking. Holloman said, and I'm pretty much quoting, 'I felt like my hair was standing up on end, and my muscles got tight all over. I ran. For a couple of weeks I didn't tell anyone, and when I did my brother said I was a fool.'

"Late Saturday night, the same week, a couple came to the jail and they were so scared the girl wouldn't get out of the car. Her boyfriend came in and reported that they had seen something run across Highway 15 and jump a high fence. Another call that night had reported something strange in the same vicinity the couple had just come from.

"A couple of deputies went out to check and just lucked up on finding tracks. The headlights of their car picked them up. They called me at home, and I was in bed asleep.

"I didn't even stop to put on my uniform, just threw on trousers and a sport shirt, and left. We got out there about daybreak and looked at the large tracks. The tracks showed only three toes. In the early morning light with those huge footprints coming out of the swamp, it was a spooky place. There were about four hundred prints extending for about the same number of yards. They came out of the woods and then re-entered.

"The pictures we took showed them clearly. So do casts of the impression. This was hard dirt and a deputy and I tried to stomp or jump and duplicate the depth those tracks had sunk into the ground. Although we each weighed over two hundred pounds, it was impossible to recreate the depth of those prints. They were about seven or eight inches wide and fourteen inches long. The distance of the stride between the tracks was from thirty-six to forty inches and the pace had a natural appearance, but that stride was far too long for any man. Near the tracks at the edge of the woods we found a heavy metal drum—its side bent in, possibly squeezed. What kind of strength it would take to do that, I can't imagine.

"Then people reported hearing weird howls and yells unlike anything heard from dogs or coyotes. By this time the local news media had written about what the Davis boy had seen, and the mangled car— I think one of the deputies talked to someone—and the wire services picked it up. Reporters were all over everywhere asking me fool questions like, 'Are you going to let some monster roam around unchecked?'

"I said, 'No, I was calling in SLED (the State Law Enforcement Division) right away.' SLED brought bloodhounds, and we went out to where the tracks were, the dogs picking up a trail, following them into the woods where they went right on trailing until they got down to the real swampy part. The man in charge of the bloodhounds said he could see that tall tree tips had been ripped off, and that something pretty big had been through there, but he had no idea what. He found saplings broken as if part of the trail had been marked. We had a bad break later that day. A cloudburst came and partially wiped out the tracks, but luckily we had taken the plaster casts first thing that morning.

"Well, within two days time the story was around the world, and in my office the phone was ringing off the hook, and I couldn't get any work done. People were calling from England, France, Germany, and heaven knows where, asking if Brown Town had an international airport." Liston Truesdale's blue eyes glinted with amusement.

"Brown Town isn't even incorporated, and the closest international airport is miles away at Greenville.

"Not only were the wire services sending reporters but so were out of state newspapers from all over the country."

He shook his head ruefully. "You wouldn't believe the traffic headache—carload after carload of people arriving in a small town like Bishopville heading out toward the swamp along Bramlett Road. A regular procession. Just curious. Hoping to see something. Television trucks were parked along the road through the swamp, their crews out hunting the beast. A one hundred million dollar reward was offered.

"It was a real ordeal. I told the media people, 'We didn't ask for this thing. This is just a small southern town, and we aren't going to be made fun of.' "

But interest did not wane quickly. Before it was over Truesdale would be appearing on Dan Rather's newscast, South Carolina Educational Television, "Good Morning America," and many other network shows. After one of these programs, the director of the Cryptozoology Museum Project at Malibu, California, Dr. Erik Beckjord, who has held this position for ten years, called the sheriff offering to try to analyze the events if he would send him the facts. Truesdale complied. Beckjord went on to conduct interviews in the area and a summation of his report follows.

Dr. Beckjord believes that what has been seen near Bishopville is a type of Bigfoot or Yeti.

According to his analysis of events, Bigfoot is known to be attracted by the smell of fish or food and also by the sound of rock music. The late hour is another factor—they tend to roam at night. Pushing a car is not unfamiliar. Jumping on it is rare. Three-fingered hands have not been reported before but seem logical when in combination with three-toed feet. Hairless Bigfoot skin has been reported by Indians in the Northwest. The green color in the Bishopville area may be algae from a swamp.

There has been some car damage in the past—an antenna was chewed on the west coast in Washington state after a Bigfoot ran into a car and scratched the top. The antenna was ripped off in the exchange and later found chewed, showing tooth marks 77 millimeters wide. The Bigfoot has been known to run with dogs and on other occasions eat dogs and coyotes. It may have chased a dog on top of the car.

The howls reported—a cross between the cries of an animal and a human—are typical of those usually reported in areas of Bigfoot activity.

It is highly unlikely that these prints were perpetrated by someone as a hoax—there is no means humanly possible to walk in a fabricated "foot set" with a stride a yard or more long for over 400 yards achieving extreme depth penetration. He would have to be seven feet tall and able to carry one thousand pounds on his back. Also, no marks were found on either side of the tracks, that is no human prints. The broken saplings are typical of a Bigfoot marking forks for others to follow. The strewing about of garbage is typical of a hungry Bigfoot. Overall, the evidence suggests that this is a Bigfoot.

Apparently Dr. Beckjord also said that the three toes and three fingers on this creature make it an extremely rare type of Bigfoot. Most are hairy and have five digits.

"After the rash of sightings and all the attention of the media," Truesdale went on, "everything quieted down and after a few months even the talk subsided. Though I had come to believe something had been in that swamp, I was grateful to finally be able to work without interruptions.

"All was quiet for about two years when on July 24, 1990, a woman called the sheriff's office to say that her car had been pursued the night before by a strange creature. I suggested she come in as soon as possible and make a statement." Truesdale began to read it aloud.

Thirty-six-year old Bertha M. Blythers from Camden, South Carolina, is an employee of Burlington Industries in Bishopville. She came in very upset early this morning, and the following interview is, as nearly as possible, in her own words.

"This past Monday night we went to my mother's house in Brown Town to pick up my son. Then we went to McDonald's to get something to eat. We left there about twenty minutes after ten and came back through Brown Town and Scape Ore Swamp. We were laughing and eating and singing and listening to the radio. In the car along with me were my son, age eighteen, my twin boys who are fourteen, my daughter, age eleven, and my five-year-old.

"As we passed the bridge I was looking straight ahead going about twenty-five miles an hour and I saw this big brown thing jump right out in front of me in the road and head for the side of the car. I quickly speeded up and steered toward the left-hand side of the road to keep whatever it was from dragging my eleven-year-old out of the car. It was a warm night and all the car windows were down."

The sheriff interrupted his reading of Mrs. Blythers' statement to say why he believed the appearance of something near her car that sounded like the stories of Lizard Man of two years ago was not a practical joke.

Too many people in a rural area like this carry guns, even high-powered rifles or Uzis, and would use one if frightened. These people would run over you first and then ask questions. Apparently whatever she saw in the road was not that familiar with a car. If you tried that as a joke around here you'd be taking your life in your hands and either be run down or shot." He went on reading her deposition.

After I turned back to the other side of the road, I mashed the brakes, slowing, and when the brake lights went on my son, Johnny, saw something walking across the road behind us. He wanted me to turn around and go back but I wouldn't, I was too scared. There was no way I would have turned that car around and gone back. My daughter was screaming, and I had to reach over and straighten her out.

I came on home and called my sister, Virginia, and told her what had happened. She said to report it to the sheriff's office immediately. I didn't want to because I thought they would think it was a joke or something. My son wanted me to go and report it right then, but instead I came on home.

I was so scared that when I got to the house, I was too scared to get out of the car, and when I did I thought I'd never find the right key to get in the door.

It was obvious that even retelling the story evoked reactions of fear all over again.

"What did it look like?" Sheriff Truesdale asked her.

"It was tall—had a chest like a human. I saw it from the waist up, but I didn't see his face. The chest was big—at least a yard wide. It almost filled that window, and what I saw of it looked like it was covered with brown hair.

"I'm not wanting to go on any TV show, Sheriff, and it wasn't my imagination. It wasn't a bear, and it was like nothing I ever saw before."

She spoke rapidly and she was very upset. The sheriff sent one of his deputies off with her to show him where it had happened.

The area wasn't far from where Chris Davis had changed his tire. According to the deputy, "The woods beside the road were covered with kudzu vines, and the shoulders on each side were grass. Of course, that meant no prints. We couldn't track anything. There really wasn't any more we could do for her." That was in 1990.

"In the middle of 1991, someone reported sighting something similar in Richland County," said Truesdale. "The Congaree River runs through a large swamp there right near Columbia. All the sightings have been near swampy areas and they have been at night. Since our own, I've heard of them in Texas, Florida, and California. In Pennsylvania there's a report of something people up there called 'the muddy man'."

He gestured toward the chest at his feet full of clippings and letters from all over the world and copies of statements from individuals.

"There's a statement that's not there that I wish I could have gotten but I understood. One of the best accounts came from a colonel in the area who is a friend of mine. He was returning from a wedding, driving back about dusk on the highway through the swamp when he saw a strange looking figure at least seven feet tall run across the road in front of his car. He braked for it but didn't stop or go back. Was he drinking? No way. It was a Baptist wedding and no drinks were served. He would have given me a formal statement but he was up for promotion to the rank of brigadier general. He talked to his attorney and the attorney said, 'You value your privacy, don't you?' Then he advised him not to make a statement if he wanted that promotion.

"I was skeptical when it all started," said the former sheriff, "but since then I have been sent so many reports of similar things in other parts of the country."

The swamp looks just as it has for centuries. It is still a dismal place where shining black ribbons of narrow waterways wind through the trees in the eerie twilight, and the forest is dark, mysterious, impenetrable, covering miles and miles of Lee County. A creature could live out there and never show itself to a human being.

For all I know someone may be seeing a creature along Brown Town road tonight," says Truesdale.

Notes

The notes that follow provide information about the sources of the stories in this collection. Some of these stories about ghosts or strange creatures have been part of my repertoire for many years and the specifics of their origins have been forgotten. A few of the sources are listed as "anonymous" at their request.

1. Angie's Dog Always

Collected from the late Dr. Gaine Cannon. Dr. Cannon and his mountain hospital—The Albert Schweitzer Memorial Hospital—were the subject of a story in *Look* magazine. The doctor's visit to a sick child in an isolated mountain cabin during a snowstorm results in an experience both startling and poignant.

2. The Hounds of Merrywood

Adapted from *Animal Ghosts or Animal Hauntings and the Hereafter* by Elliott O'Donnell. (London: William Rider & Son, LTD 1913). The dogs are the "avenging hounds" pursuing the murderer to bring retribution.

3. Captain Kidd's Farewell

Collected from Mrs. Julie Stanley Kidd of Gastonia, North Carolina, on January 4, 1994.

4. The Ghost at Wickersham Hall

Adapted from *Animal Ghosts or Animal Hauntings and the Hereafter* by Elliott O'Donnell (London: William Rider & Son, Ltd, 1913). This story was of the period when interest in psychic phenomena was prevalent in England. It contains many of the archetypal images of the tragic vision of the world, like the desolate wilderness area on the way

157

from Wickersham station to the house which is remniscent of the sinister forest in Milton's *Comus*, or in the beginning of Dante's *Inferno*.

5. The Ponies of Tule Canyon

Provided by the Manuscript Division, Library of Congress, for which the basic elements of this story were recorded on January 18, 1936. Texas native Mrs. Kim Teter, who had heard the story of the phantom horses all her life, confirmed the general details of the story. Historic detail comes from several sources including the Amarillo, Texas *Globe-News*, September 22, 1974. The Rodgers ranch was at the mouth of Tule Canyon.

6. The Ghost of Vallecito

Collected from an unidentified source at the public library in San Diego, California, before 1993. Ghost stories seem to abound concerning early stagecoach stops like the one at Vallecito just as old stagecoach inns, taverns and even lighthouses often became a focal point for ghost stories. The ghostly guardian of a treasure is typical. Another version of this story was published in W.A. Bailey's *Golden Mirages* (New York: Macmillan, 1941).

7. The Black Pig

Adapted from a story provided by the Manuscript Division, the Illinois WPA file, Library of Congress. The field worker was Roper Harrison of Alton, Illinois, who recorded the basic facts on September 21, 1936. His sources were W. Skinner, Wm. Stopkotle, Emma Spurgeon and L.P. Frothhardt. A crime in Germany starts a chain of events leading to a weird retribution for an immigrant family in Illinois. This is another story of retribution.

8. Stubborn as a Mule

Retold after a telephone interview in February 1994 with Mrs. Lois Goodson, Edwards County, Illinois Historical Society. This is an old folk tale of Edwards County based on the first Brissenden to settle in the area. Additional details on the Brissenden family came from Mrs. Goodson and the Albion, Illinois town clerk. Among the previously published versions are M.A. Jagendorf's *Sand in the Bag*, B.A. Botkin's *A Treasury of New England Folklore*, and Patricia Clyne Edwards' *Strange and Supernatural Animals*.

9. Stampede Mesa

Adapted from stories found in the the Texas Works Progress Administration file, Manuscript Division, Library of Congress. Other factual information came from the *Globe-News*, Amarillo, Texas. A very good ghost story, one of a variety of legends surrounding this mesa, has been published in *Ghost Stories of the American Southwest*, by Richard and Judy Dockrey Young (Little Rock: August House Publishers, 1991).

10. Alfie

Adapted from Tom Welch's *Ghosts of Polk County* (Fort Madison: Quixote Press, 1988) with the permission of publisher Bruce Carlson, with factual information on hog raising in the early 1900s contributed by Palmer Holden at Iowa State University, Animal Science Extension. This is somewhat reminiscent of *Charlotte's Web* by E.B. White. The inevitable demise of the pig is central to most folklore stories involving this animal.

11. The Omen

Adapted from a story provided by the Manuscript Division, the Arkansas WPA file, Library of Congress. The source of the incident was James Waid, Confederate veteran from Malvern, Arkansas. In Shakespeare the hooting of an owl is used to convey the most ominous of warnings. The same connotations were attributed to the owl's hoots by American Indians and the early western European settlers.

12. Prowler of the Cumberlands

Adapted from an account in the Tennessee WPA file, Manuscript Division, Library of Congress. This account was related by Robert Potter, Robert Wheeler, and others. The newspaper clippings from the March 1908 *Pittsburgh Hustler*, Pittsburgh, Tennessee, about a "strange animal" were provided by Whitwell, Tennessee regional historian Eulene Harris.

13. The Plat-eye

Adapted from a story provided by the Manuscript Division, the South Carolina WPA file, Library of Congress, Mrs. G.W. Chandler, Murrell's Inlet, South Carolina, June 17, 1936; also by an interview with Daisy Scott Brown, Edisto Island, South Carolina, March 1993. This is a supernatural, much-feared creature of the coastal plains of South

Carolina and Georgia. Stories about plat-eyes have been told since Colonial days. There are those who believe the plat-eye, taking on a variety of animal shapes, possesses a human spirit. Navajo lore has a similar belief.

14. Warren the Werewolf

Collected in 1989 from a high school boy living in a rural area of North Carolina, north of Greensboro.

15. The Jersey Devil

Collected from a telephone interview with David Wilcox, branch manager of the Atlantic County Public Library West, Hammonton, N.J. (the county in which Leeds Point is located) along with information from the following sources:

> Beck, Henry Charlton, *Jersey Genesis: The Story of the Mullica River* (New Brunswick: Rutgers University Press, 1983).
>
> Boucher, Jack E., *Absegami Yesterday* (Atlantic County Historical Society, 1963).
>
> *A Brief History of the New Jersey Pinelands*, The Pinelands Commission, New Lisbon, N.J. (P.O. Box 7, New Lisbon, NJ 08064).
>
> McMahon, William, *South Jersey Towns: History and Legend* (New Brunswick: Rutgers University Press, 1973).
>
> McCloy, James F. and Miller, Ray, Jr., *The Jersey Devil* (Wallingford: The Middle Atlantic Press, 1976).
>
> Young, Eugene V. and Abrahamson, Elaine Conover, *The Story of Galloway Township* (Galloway Township Bicentennial Committee, 1976).

Coverage of the story also ran in *Hammonton News, Atlantic City Press, New York Times, Newark Star Ledger, Philadelphia Inquirer, The Record* (Paulsboro, N.J.) *Salem Sunbeam*, and *Woodbury Daily Times*.

16. Ogopogo the Sea Monster

Collected from Arlene Gaal in British Columbia, who is the local expert on Ogopogo. This story is based on an interview with Ms. Gaal and, with her permission, contains references to selected sightings as related in her book, *Ogopogo*, published in Canada (Surrey: Hancock House, 1931).

17. The Lizard Man

Collected from Liston Truesdale, former sheriff of Lee County, at Bishopville, South Carolina, on December 28, 1993. I also consulted newspaper stories, chief among them those from the nearby Sumter, South Carolina *Daily Item*.